I0626862

TRIA ELLINKA

A Trio of Greek Goddess Tragedies

KATE SEGER

Copyright © 2021 Tria' Ellinka'

Written by: Kate Seger

Cover Design by: Lauren Hanson

Published by: Tarina Anthologies

ISBN:

This is a work of fiction. All characters, organizations, and events portrayed
are either products of the author's imagination or used fictitiously.

✵ Created with Vellum

❧ I ❧

ECHOES

I REMEMBER THE WAY SUNLIGHT SPLASHED ACROSS HIS FACE, dappling it with shadow. We met in this forest amid the stands of fir and pine that have swathed Mount Kithairon since the dawn of days. This vale, my home, and my captivity for eternity, the realm to which Hera banished me for my 'lust'.

After she stole my words, of course.

Never mind that it was Zeus who forced himself upon me, who cajoled and wheedled his way into my arms and my heart. I was an Oread. Treacherous seduction was bred in my immortal blood. Who would believe that I was not to blame?

Certainly not Hera.

If Zeus was my first mistake, Narcissus was my greatest. I should have known better than to reveal myself to a man in this wood. This is a cursed place, a place that exists solely for my chastisement, from what I can tell. It was reckless of me. Did I really believe that Hera and the Fates would allow me to be happy?

I was a fool.

It began on a day like so many others. Humdrum in its

tedium. The forest whispering its secrets. Me, listening, unable to respond. Swallowing back the forgotten words hovering just on the tip of my tongue, tormenting me, and kissing the leaves with my sighs.

Until I set eyes on Narcissus. He stalked my forest, sleek, sinuous, and feline. I hung back, following him for days as he trespassed upon my sacred ground before I dared approach. Silently I prowled, keeping my lithe body reed-thin, pressing against the trunks of the trees, trusting them to keep me hidden.

I watched by night as he stretched out his sculpted form and rested in the flickering glow of his campfire. I admired him by day, which was when he was at his loveliest. It was summer, and he was often bare-chested, beads of sweat glistening upon the fine golden hairs on his breast.

I was drawn to him.

So, like the fool I am, I threw caution to the wind.

Narcissus was standing in a small clearing, bow held aloft. His arrow was sighted on a whitetail gazelle, one eye squinting, the other bright and blue as a mountain pool. His skin gleamed golden in the afternoon light, a tangle of sandy blonde hair windswept away from his face.

I wanted him to see me, to know me, to love me.

That is the nature of an Oread, after all, or so I've been told; to long for, and to yearn to be longed for.

It is also, I believe, the nature of love.

I stepped out from behind the sheltering arms of a majestic sentinel tree. The intentional rustle of brush drew his eye, distracted him long enough for the doe to bound off gracefully through the underbrush. This pleased me. The creatures who walked beneath the sheltering boughs of this glade were the closest things to friends I had.

At first, his finely chiseled face was carved into a mask of irritation, his eyes narrowed, aquiline nose held high aloft, jaw clenched. Then, slowly, he recognized me for what I was.

I should tell you, I am no great beauty amongst the Gods. I have seen Aphrodite with her golden flowing locks, rosebud lips, and pearlescent skin emanating seduction like a beacon. That is not who I am. I am only Echo, a mountain nymph, a small goddess. But I have wiles of my own, and I am not without my charms.

"Greetings," he finally said. His voice was a warm baritone.

His gaze turned admiring as it roved over my body. I gnawed my lower lip, feeling uncomfortable with my nakedness on full display. It had been so long since I had consorted with another sentient being. I felt feral in his presence.

"Greetings," I mimicked back, my frustration mounting. My voice was a flat breathy thing, and I winced at the sound of it. I, Echo, who used to lure men into my arms with a song, now had no words of my own. I could only throw back those uttered at me.

"I hope I do not trespass upon your forest, lady?" he asked smoothly, eyebrow arching.

"Forest," I murmured, a flush creeping into my cheeks. I smiled weakly, hoping to appear welcoming, and prayed I didn't look quite the fool I felt. Trembling, I took a few small steps closer.

I tapped myself on the chest, steeling myself and speaking the one word of my own that Hera had left me. "Echo," – my name.

Hearing it upon my own lips, I felt a flicker of the girl I had once been rekindling. I struck what I hoped was an alluring pose. I was, after all, a nymph. Seduction was in my blood. So Hera had said, so Zeus had claimed. If I wanted this man, I would have him.

"Narcissus," he returned.

My smile began to feel a bit more natural, so I beckoned to him. His lips quirked up, amused. He moved towards me with long, confidant strides. He opened his mouth to speak, but I drew a finger to my lips. I would have him silent, as I was forced to be. Taking his large, calloused hands in mine, I drew them first to my lips, kissing each knuckle, then placing them on my shoulders.

He understood.

Tracing my collar bone, he skimmed his fingers over my breasts, circling my navel, then planting his hands firmly on my hips. There was hunger in his eyes. I drew my tongue slowly over my lips.

He pulled me down onto the pine needle carpet of the forest floor. The soft hummus of leaf and earth cushioned me as he loomed above me.

And then he took me.

Perhaps it was a kind of revenge. Zeus had ravaged me, tricked and deceived me, then left me to Hera's mercy. Yet, after all those long years, I still had some small power of my own. So I used it to seduce Narcissus, as Zeus had done to me.

Afterward, we lay in the twilight, my body curled against his as the sky shifted from bright scarlet to the purple of a bruise. He whispered endearments into my ear, curled long tendrils of my hair around his fingers. When we awoke, the sun was high in the sky, but it was a softer, gentler sun as if Helios had chosen to take pity on me as I lay in Narcissus' embrace.

So it was that he came to spend a season in my forest. We walked the woodland trails side by side. I showed him the hidden places where waterfalls caught the light just so, forming shimmering rainbows, and the dens where fox pups tumbled with one another.

Narcissus chattered endlessly. I could only respond in

clipped mimicry, but I listened to his every word. He told me of his parents, his father Cephissus, a river God, his mother Liriope, a nymph, like myself. He spoke only of himself, but I did not mind. I had lived so long in a world without words; each one was like a drop of water after years of drought.

I wanted him to stay forever. I knew that he could not. Even if things had been different, he would have tired of me. Narcissus did not love me. He loved only himself. The bright beauty of our passion was destined to fade. But I, headstrong and happy, refused to think on that.

I cannot say how long we shared this enchanted forest. Time moves differently in the realm of the Gods. It was long enough that I grew to know and cherish his every expression. The way his jaw muscle twitched when he concentrated, how his smile spread slow and lazy across his face. The only place I dared not bring him was my pool. I knew Hera had placed a heavy enchantment upon that spot. I did not know the nature of the foul spell she had cast and did not wish to. Whenever Narcissus drew near it, I would tug on his arm and lead him away.

Then one day, when the leaves had exchanged their green summer gowns for those of red and gold, I awoke to find him gone. The autumn air had turned cold overnight, and Boreas, the north wind, hissed in my ears, lashing me with his tongue. I waited for what felt like an eternity, shivering and silently begging every God in Olympia to return my love to me.

But the Gods had long been deaf to me. Hera made sure of that. How can one's pleas be heard when one has no voice?

I searched the forest until there was but one place left to look. Fear coiled in my belly as I dragged myself towards the enchanted pool. It was a secluded spot, deep in the woodlands. But Narcissus knew this forest nearly as well as I by then. Perhaps he'd noticed my trickery, my attempts to lead him away from the spot. I never imagined it would pique his curiosity, and he would venture there on his own.

I cursed Hera. If only I had my words, I could have warned him away, explained why we dare not enter that one glade.

Padding quickly across the rock-strewn path, I was clumsy in my terror, wondering if there was still time to sway him from this folly.

I bounded into the clearing where the river fanned out into a wide pool. Trees bowed their heads around the spot, casting shadows over the still waters. I breathed a sigh of relief when I saw him perched upon the bank, gazing calmly into the water as lily pads drifted by. Naive as I was, I thought him safe from whatever evil Hera had cast out upon this place.

I was wrong. I was a fool to believe either of us would be spared her wrath.

Moving to where Narcissus knelt, I tugged at his arm gently at first, then harder. He brushed me aside as if I were a gnat, an irritation. I ran my fingers through his coils of fair hair, tenderly at first. By then, it had grown to his shoulders, and when he ignored my gentle touch, I tugged fiercely at his locks. Still, he did not glance away from the surface of the pool.

Panic formed a lump threatening to choke the breath out of my silent throat. I peered into the pool to see what it was that held him so rapt. Bemused, I realized it was only his own reflection. Yet he gazed at it with a longing that had never been there when he looked upon me, not even in the throes of our lovemaking.

Desperate, I yanked his face towards mine, forcing him to meet my eyes. He cursed and spat like a quarrelsome feline. A glob of spittle stuck to my cheek.

"Foul witch," he muttered with such disgust etched into

his face that tears sprang to my eyes. My tears had no effect. He returned his gaze to the still waters.

I threw my head back and howled wordlessly at the sky, at Hera, at Olympus. How dare they take from me the only thing I held dear in my pathetic eternal life?

Narcissus did not speak to me again after that. He never again met my gaze or touched his lips to mine. Every day I silently raged and did all within my power to return him to his senses, to draw him away from the rapture of his own reflection.

Nothing worked.

His golden beauty slowly withered, and I could only watch. I brought him all the delicacies the forest had to offer to tempt him. He shunned the soft earthy mushroom caps we had once devoured together. Ignored the last dwindling blackberries that I pricked my fingers on thorns to forage for him.

Still, he stared at his reflection as if it were his one true love.

Autumn came and went, leaves falling dead and brown from the trees to drift listlessly in the pool. Never did they obscure my lover's reflection. The enchantment held him fast.

Then came the day I pushed aside the ferns and did not see Narcissus. I had to stop my heart from leaping. My first instinct was that he had freed himself from the vile spell. A futile hope. By then, he was a husk of what he had once been, an immortal decaying to nothing before my eyes. He lacked the power to rise from his place on the shore.

Still, 1 loved him dearly and clung to that last wisp of hope. I would have cared for him for eternity if the Gods allowed it.

The Gods, of course, would allow no such thing.

I cannot say whether Hera knew what trap she was laying

when she cursed the pool. Perhaps she wished only to trap me. We Oreads are known for our vanity. This, too, they say, is in our blood. The punishment she meted out was far worse.

Or maybe it was not Hera at all. It could be Narcissus had brought this, somehow, upon himself. Had been led to my glade, to this pool, by the wicked wiles of the Fates themselves.

I will never know.

I crept into the clearing, knowing what I would find. Narcissus' body, emaciated, aged a hundred years, floated facedown in the algae. Tears slid down my cheeks, mingling with the waters of the cursed pool.

When I was finally able to will myself to do the deed, I pulled his body from the water and laid him down amid the reeds. I smoothed his wet hair, now gone white as bone, back from his brow, then closed his cloudy blue eyes, once so clear, and folded his skeletal arms across his cadaverous chest.

I had nowhere to go. And so here I remain. Holding vigil over my lost lover's bones. Silent until the long, high, keening cry builds up inside, and I can contain it no more.

I am nothing now but a cry in the night. An echo in the forest. Warning others away from this cursed pool.

❀ II ❀
SCYLLA

MY NAME IS SCYLLA, THOUGH FEW CALL ME BY IT NOW. IT is a name from a time when I was a sea nymph, beautiful and favored by Poseidon, frolicking in my family's watery halls. Scylla is the last shred of a bygone era when my days were spent wandering amid tidepools, collecting conch shells, and riding the breaking waves to shore.

Now that I am a monster, men call me the beast of the narrow strait, if they think of me at all. I do my best to live up to their expectations, to act the part of a bloodthirsty sea creature. I snatch a handful of foolish mortals from the prows of their ships with my great tentacled arms. I dash their frail bodies against the rocks, then drag them down to consume deep in the sea caves I call home.

Sailors ought to be grateful when it's me they come across. Charybdis, whose lair lies across the strait from mine, would sink their whole bloody boat and eat the lot of them. But I don't have the heart of a killer; I do not enjoy doing it. I consume them only to appease the great cavernous hunger in me. The only blood I lust for is the blood of those who turned me into the thing I am today.

Circe, that vile jealous witch, with her potions and her poisons. Glaucus, that cocky, up-jumped mortal with his ridiculous fishtail. When I crush men's bones in my tentacles, it is their faces I see in my mind's eye.

But I'm getting ahead of myself.

Every tragic tale starts somewhere, and mine begins on a sunny day in midsummer. The Aegean sparkled like a tourmaline. Dolphins dawdled near the surface, chittering as they crested waves while seabirds traced lazy circles in the cloud-banded sky.

I frequented a sheltered cove in those days, with great rocks worn flat by the insistent caress of the sea. I liked to linger there on the surface, letting the sun kiss my skin. I would lie on those rocks for hours, just watching the clouds above paint pictures in the sky.

On that ill-fated day, I was not the only one who had the idea of bathing in the sun's warm rays. When I arrived at the cove, he was already there. I knew him at a glance. Tall and broad-shouldered, built like a sailor, but with a massive scintillating fishtail. Glaucus. The mortal made God after eating a magical herb.

I was not a gossip like my sisters. I kept to myself in my father's halls, but it was impossible not to hear the tales of Glaucus, the newly minted prophet and Sea God. I had seen him roving about on dozens of occasions. And I had seen the way the other nymph's eyes followed him at feasts and parties. Circe, that strange dark daughter of Helios, in particular, seemed taken by him. If I had known the history between them, I likely would not have crawled up onto those rocks and batted the lashes of my pretty Oceanid blue eyes. Circe had always frightened me. I would never have invited her wrath.

But I did not know, so up I crawled.

"Beautiful day," he said, his tone mild. He continued staring at the sky until I answered.

"It is my Lord Glaucus. I love being above on days like this," I said with a coy smile.

Glaucus turned to look at me when I spoke his name. He wore an expression of curiosity as his eyes, green and gold, mottled like sea glass, appraised me. His beard was forked, and his face more weathered than the unblemished skin of those born Gods.

"You're one of the nymphs. My apologies, there are just so many of you, I haven't placed a name with every face."

"I am Scylla," I replied, trying to keep the disappointment from my voice. I was widely considered one of the most beautiful nymphs, and he ought to have known me.

"Ah! Yes, Triton's daughter. You know, the tales of your beauty do not come close to what I see before me, Scylla." He shot me a roguish grin, making color rise in my cheeks.

"My Lord Glaucus is kind," I murmured.

"I can be." His eyes twinkled as he flashed a lascivious look at me. My heart beat a little faster and my palms began to sweat.

"So, do you come here often?" I asked and immediately felt a fool—a silly little nymph.

Glaucus only laughed and shook his head, golden curls swirling in the sunlight. "First time. I'm still learning the lay of the land."

I smiled at him. "I'd be happy to show you some of my haunts," I offered. "There are lovely caves to the west where the sea has carved the stone as if it were made of crystal, and there are sea kelp gardens to the east that the Merfolk tend." I bit my lip, worried I was carrying on like a foolish child.

He studied me for a few moments with an unreadable expression on his face. He seemed intrigued but also... hesitant.

"I should like that Scylla, daughter of Triton. You can call on me anytime," he finally replied.

❧ 2 ❧

I DID CALL ON HIM. GLAUCUS HAD A MASSIVE PALACE erected on the seabed, a cavernous place of fossilized stone, vibrant with anemones and living coral. It was beautiful and luxurious. The type of palace any nymph might dream of calling her home. Glaucus and I would meet twice a week at dawn, embarking upon all manner of adventures. I won't bore you with the details of each escapade, for I hold the memories of those days close. They are sweet yet bitter and not for the ears of mere mortals.

Then came the day when I arrived at Glaucus's palace and chanced upon Circe. As I said, she and I had never gotten on. She might have been the daughter of the Sun God, but she was a darkling creature, always fussing with strange magicks.

Glaucus had by then enchanted me with his wit, his worldliness, his tales of the cities and fields and forests of the mortal realm, places I had never ventured to and could hardly imagine. There was a gruffness to him that I found alluring. Bold and brazen, the man who'd become a God had captured my poor stupid heart.

So it was that when I arrived at Glaucus's gates just as

Circe was leaving, I vowed not to be intimidated by her. Who was she, but another nymph, like me, and a far less beautiful one? With her dark lank hair and sallow skin, her cold eyes, surely Glaucus could not care for her as he did for me.

"Hail, Scylla," Circe greeted me.

"Circe." I gave her a curt nod. She narrowed her eyes at me, and I felt sure the water around us grew a bit colder.

"What brings you to Glaucus's doorstep?" Her tone was casual, but there was a layer of ice underneath it. She was plainly not pleased by my presence there. Fortunately, Glaucus arrived and put an end to the awkward interaction.

"Circe, Scylla, my two favorite nymphs! How nice to see you both together," Glaucus boomed, propelling himself towards us with his powerful fishtail.

Circe and I exchanged glances, then she wrinkled up her small, pointed nose. "Thank you for your company this morning, Glaucus. I hope you find the potion beneficial. I must be going," she replied stiffly, not taking her eyes off me.

It was all I could do not to tremble beneath the weight of her black-eyed gaze.

"Yes, well, thank you, Circe. Come Scylla, what's on our agenda for today?" Glaucus draped his muscular arm over my shoulder. I watched as Circe's face paled to bone white, and her pinched expression tightened even further.

With Glaucus' arm around me, I felt brazen.

"Oh, there are lovely caves called the lover's hideaway. Have you seen them yet?" I asked, turning away from Circe's burning glare to blink prettily up at Glaucus.

He arched his thick eyebrows and let out a guffaw.

"The lover's hideaway, eh? Sounds like just the place I'm in the mood for," Glaucus rumbled.

I giggled. When I turned again, Circe was gone; only a trail of bubbles left her wake.

Good, I thought unkindly. What business did a sour-faced

witch like Circe have interfering in my blossoming love affair? Glaucus would never take a nymph like her to the lover's hideaway. Circe, daughter of Helios, was no threat to me.

It hadn't occurred to me, then, that Circe's dabbling in herbs and potions might be more than just a way to pass the time. She had not yet begun turning men into lions and swine. If I had known what she was capable of, perhaps I would have been a bit more discreet in my pursuit of Glaucus. Maybe I would have been kinder to her. But I was young and a fool of a nymph.

So, we ventured out to the lover's hideaway. That was the day Glaucus took me amid the crystalline stalactites. I had been with men before, of course. Nymphs are not known for their chastity. But it was different with Glaucus. Once I got past the flopping fishtail, which I admit was a bit peculiar, he brought me quickly to a rapturous climax.

I believed this was the beginning of something beautiful as we lay in each other's arms, surrounded by the pink and red anemones that gave the caves their name. Glaucus and I would be wed. I would move into his grand palace and away from the incessant twittering of my sisters. We would have beautiful children, who would hopefully take after me, for I did not want Piscean offspring.

I was full of dreams of the future.

I had no idea those dreams would turn out to be the stuff of nightmares. That even as we spoke, Circe had begun to concoct a plan that would change everything.

3

TIDEPOOLS. I HAD ALWAYS BEEN FOND OF THEM. AS children, nymphs are often brought to the pools to splash and play in the sunlight while their mothers are off seducing mortals with their siren songs. Most grow out of such things as they get older, spending more time beneath the waves than above them, leaving the shore to the mortals.

Not I.

Nearly every morning when I rose if the sun was shining and I did not have a date with Glaucus, I would venture to the tide pools. I loved the rub of the sand and stones beneath my toes. I loved gazing into the miniature worlds that existed in the waters trapped by the withdrawing tide. Sand crabs and minnows, starfish and urchins, all displaced yet not. It fascinated me to watch their existence in these microcosms, suspended there until the sea swept them back to their everyday lives.

Circe and I had grown up together. Had splashed and laughed and played in these very pools. Well, perhaps *she* had not laughed and played. Even as a girl, Circe had always been dour. She never wished to join in the games of the Nymphs.

She was always off gathering weeds and drawing strange symbols on rocks.

She must have recalled how taken I was by the pools and known I still frequented them, for that was where she chose to spring her trap.

The water was about knee-deep. I was crouched, inspecting an octopus who'd made his temporary home between two large rocks, when I heard a strange dissonant humming behind me. I turned, and there she stood. She looked less sullen than usual. Her thin lips were quirked into something like a smile, but it did not reach her eyes, and there was a menacing edge to her expression that immediately made me wary.

"Circe, what a pleasant surprise. I did not know you still came to the pools," I greeted her, tossing my platinum locks. I don't know what I hoped to accomplish with this preening. Intimidating her with my beauty in the face of her plainness could not have helped my cause.

"I don't often," she admitted. "This was a special trip. A certain plant I sought can be found here." She still wore that strange smile, which did not reach her eyes. "Would you like to see what I've found?" She stepped closer to the pool where I knelt.

I shook my head and laughed.

"Oh no, Circe, you know I neither know nor care about plants like you do. Not that there's anything wrong with plants, I'm just not so worldly and knowledgeable as you. They aren't my... cup of tea." I was trying to win her over by deferring to her superior intellect, hoping she might leave me in peace, but it clearly wasn't working. She continued stalking slowly towards me, her hands cupped and extended before her.

"It is for Glaucus," she said, and this piqued my interest,

though I could not say whether I was intrigued or concerned. Perhaps a bit of both.

"For Glaucus?" I echoed.

"I don't know about you, but I find that fishtail of his revolting," she said in a conspiratorial tone.

I laughed at that. The thought certainly had crossed my mind. As I've said, I found the idea of Piscean offspring abhorrent. I wanted my children to be nymphs, not fish.

"These herbs can bring about a metamorphosis." She sat down upon a rock beside me, dipping her toes into the pool. "Here, I'll show you. You see that octopus there?" Circe pointed to the octopus clinging to the underbelly of the rocks. "Just think about octopus for a moment. Odd creatures, aren't they? With those tentacles always flailing about grasping at things. Forever forced to resort to hugging rocks, so they don't get swept away by the current. Even a fishtail is surely preferable to that."

This is the point in the story where you will realize that I truly am a great fool. Perhaps the greatest fool the world has ever known. For when Circe told me to think about the octopus, that is precisely what I did. I assumed she would be performing some sort of magic upon it. Perhaps giving it a fishtail.

As I stared at the creature, I saw her release the herbs she held from the corner of my eye. They drifted down, as if in slow motion, until they landed in the pool.

Then Circe began to laugh.

At first, I did not understand what was happening. I cocked my head at her, bewildered. Then I felt a sickening plunge in my belly, the feeling of being caught in open water during a storm. After a few moments, the peculiar sensation of my bones shifting beneath my skin. It wasn't painful so much as it was odd, disorienting. A roar broke out in my skull, drowning out Circe's laughter. I pressed my hands to my ears, but they felt strange, not like hands at all. I fell to the ground, my legs no longer able to bear my own weight. My skull cracked against the rock where the little octopus had been hiding.

The world went dark.

❧ 4 ❧

I MUST HAVE BEEN UNCONSCIOUS FOR SOME TIME, FOR WHEN I woke, it was full dark. Circe was gone. A crescent moon veiled in clouds frowned down at me. I tried to sit up, but my body would not obey me. It was like I wore a skin that wasn't my own.

Then I saw it. Floating in the tide pool, over-spilling onto the rocks. An enormous purple tentacle where my leg should have been. I moved what ought to have been my hand. Another tentacle, this once with a great pincer-like a crab. My breaths came unevenly as I drew this phantom limb over my body. Where once my perfectly flat belly had been, I felt a mound of gelatinous flesh.

No, I thought. Circe would not - could not - do this to me. Yes, she had ways with herbs and magic, but to turn me into this monstrosity? With just a handful of flower petals? Impossible. For a moment, I just floundered there, torn between terror and fury.

Eventually, I dragged myself down the beach towards the tide line. It was slow going in my huge, unwieldy body, and after a time, I could drag myself no more. I lay there, panting in the moonlight like some beached thing, the sea lapping at me until the tide rose, at last high enough to sweep me up and carry me back into the ocean's depths.

I should, perhaps, have gone first to my father, Triton. He was a Sea God, and he might've put Circe in her place, ordered her to change me back. Or perhaps not. My father had many daughters and disliked getting involved with Helios' brood. What was the loss of just one nymph when there were so many others?

I'll never know what my father might have done, for I didn't seek his aid. Instead, I fled for Glaucus's palace. He, too, was a Sea God, and he loved me. Or so I thought. Perhaps he might have some magic to turn me back. If not, surely he would order Circe to do so once he'd seen what the witch had done to me.

But when I made my laborious way to his palace, Glaucus stood before the locked gates with Circe at his side. The look on his face was one of pure disgust as I pulled myself along with my unwieldy appendages.

"I know what you've done, Scylla," he said, mouth turned down in a grim frown. Circe stood with her eyes downcast, that same small, strange smile pulling at her lips.

"What I've done?" I demanded. "Look at what she's done! She's turned me into a monster!" My voice trembled with righteous indignation as I pointed what should have been a slender finger but was instead a beefy purple tentacle at Circe. I could not believe my eyes when Glaucus stepped protectively in front of her and glowered at me.

"Lying will not help your case, Scylla. Circe has told me all. How you longed for the comforts of my palace but did not wish to risk your children being born 'grotesque' like me, with a fish's tail. How you went to her demanding a potion that would make my physique more to your liking." He spat the words at me, and I could do nothing but stare at him, agog.

"Glaucus, I never—" I began, but Glaucus barreled on.

"I know how she confronted you at the pools and tried to talk you out of this folly. How you tried to take the elixir from her by force. How your insistence left her no choice but to drop her herbs into the water, turning you into this," he waved his hand and shuddered in disgust, "this monster that stands before us now."

Hot tears burst from my eyes, but they were black as ink when they hit the water. I choked on a sob as Circe looked up, her eyes hard and shiny as onyx. Not a hint of remorse in them. She would not change me back. Not willingly.

"Glaucus," I pleaded. "Please listen. That is not how this came about."

"Save your tears, Scylla. It is not Glaucus you need to convince. It's our fathers." Circe waved a bony hand at me. She was so thin, barely more than skin stretched tight over her bones. But there was power in that frail body of hers. Great power.

With that single gesture, a large golden cage sprang up around me. I was well and truly trapped.

Glaucus and Circe carried my cage to my father's halls, deaf to my pleas that they release me and change me back at once.

THEY PLACED THE GILDED CAGE IN THE CENTER OF THE Great Hall, the same massive chamber where I had once feasted and flirted. The hall was empty, but for my own family and Circe's, and with so few occupants, the space suddenly seemed massive, hollow, and intimidating. My fellow nymph sisters and cousins gathered around my prison, flitting about, chirping, and giggling as they peered between the bars of my enclosure. I cowered in one corner, wrapping my tentacles around my bloated body, inky black tears streaming down my cheeks.

"Is that really Scylla?"

"So they say."

"Circe did this to her?"

"That is what Circe claims. She was planning to cast a wicked spell on Glaucus."

"Can you imagine? How hideous she is. Will your father make Circe change her back?"

"*Can* Circe change her back?"

"I prefer her like this, don't you? Much more interesting."

Neither my mother nor Circe's were present. This made sense. Someone would be punished here, and our fathers did not want the matrons about wailing and weeping and wringing their hands. But I would have given anything to have my mother by my side, assuring me things would be alright, hushing my sisters and brothers and cousins.

The chatter abruptly ceased, and the nymphs dispersed, drawing back from my cage. I knew without seeing that my father had entered the hall. Single file, the men who would decide my fate marched up onto the dais. My father, Triton, the Sea God, Circe's father, Helios, whose bright chariot daily pulled the sun across the sky. They were indeed taking this seriously to pull Helios from his duties. Beside him, Aëetes, Circe's cold-eyed eldest brother, near as strange as she was, though a good bit fairer to gaze upon. He would rule his own kingdom soon, and as such, was ever-present when matters of state were discussed. In the rear strode Glaucus. Dear Glaucus, who I feared would be lost to me now, no matter the result of this trial. Circe's sly tongue had turned him from my lover to my enemy.

Aëetes studied me, dispassionate, with cool calculation in his eyes. Assessing his sister's handiwork as if I were a sculpture she had carved, not a young nymph trapped in this monstrous body. It was he who spoke first, though he did not direct his words at me.

"Sweet sister," he said with a sharp bark of laughter. "This is fine work. I didn't realize the true nature of your skills. To leave that pretty face amongst those five monstrous heads. And the tentacles with the grasping crab claws. That is a nice touch."

Circe, who had floated over to place herself between my cage and the men, bowed her head. A demure acceptance of her brother's praise.

She did not hesitate to begin pleading her case. "Father, good Lords of the Sea," she began, subdued. "Before you reprimand me, understand, I did not undertake this lightly." Her dark eyes glistened like flecks of jet as she raked them over the men then settled them to rest upon me in my cage.

I cannot say whether there was fury or desperation in my gaze when my eyes met hers. Whatever she saw there, it did nothing to sway her from her course. She told her tale, manufactured from start to finish. I watched frowns of displeasure bloom on the faces of the men as she spoke. By the time she had finished weaving her web of deception, and I was called on to speak in my defense, I knew it was futile. Their minds were made up.

Still, I had to try.

"Father," I addressed my plea to Triton. If any of these men would give me the benefit of the doubt, surely it would be my own father. "Circe does not speak the truth."

Helios bristled. "Does your wicked scheming child call my daughter a liar?" he demanded, his face turning bright red with rage.

I flinched, covering my eyes to block out the incandescent light the Sun God emanated, then protested, "She came to the tide pools bearing flower petals, intent on doing this to me with no provocation. There was no elixir. I never requested such a potion to use on Lord Glaucus. It was Circe who told me I might be able to change his form."

I realized my mistake immediately. I *had* wanted to change Glaucus from his piscine form. My traitorous tongue had betrayed me into an admission of guilt.

Aëetes eyebrows shot up.

"Flower petals?" Aëetes asked. "You expect us to believe my sister did this metamorphosis using only flower petals?"

I saw Circe open her mouth to speak, then slam it shut,

straining against the desire to defend her skill. Had Aëetes said this intentionally to make her backtrack on her story? If that had been his intent, it hadn't worked. Circe shot him a black look but didn't contradict her own tale to defend her skill with magic.

My father cleared his throat and glanced from Circe to myself. "I have heard enough," he said. There was a gentleness in his eyes that I did not expect, and when he spoke again, I was sure it would be to offer me a reprieve.

"Scylla, did you know you were my favorite of Crataeis's brood? You were the most beautiful, to be sure. But beauty is nothing special in a nymph. You were more than a great beauty. You were inquisitive, savvy, you thought for yourself."

I did not like that he was speaking about me in the past tense.

"And perhaps I should have suppressed that tendency in you. A nymph ought not to be plotting and scheming. She ought to be enchanting and pleasing. Perhaps this is all my fault," Triton finished with a sigh.

I recognized, with my father's great world-weary sigh, that it was over. He did not believe my story, or if he did, he did not believe it was worth the effort of going to battle with Helios to defend me.

Circe had won.

"We ought to kill her! Cut off her tentacles and feed her to the sharks in pieces!" Helios bellowed.

To his credit, my father did blanch and grimace at this suggestion. But he did not contradict the Sun God. Nor did Glaucus, who only stood with his arms crossed over his barrel chest, still wearing a scowl. To my surprise, it was Aëetes who came to my defense.

"Come now, father. What harm has Scylla truly done? My dear sweet sister foiled her plan, and Glaucus was not injured by any potion – or petals." His eyes twinkled as he looked at me. Strange eyes that shifted in hue from steel gray to indigo. Eyes that were unreadable and difficult to trust. "Let us not be hasty and punish her with death. I have another idea that ought to satisfy all parties."

My future, my very life, hinged on Aëetes, Circe's dark, unsettling brother's plan.

❦ 6 ❦

I MIGHT AS WELL HAVE LET THEM FEED ME TO THE SHARKS.

At the time, I thought Aëetes' plan to deliver me to the straits in this wretched body was a kindness. There, he said, I might seek the companionship of Charybdis. A victim of an ancient curse, he too was a sea monster now, dwelling in a cave across the channel. My banishment would serve to appease Glaucus and Helios, but perhaps I might find a friend in Charybdis. It would, Aëetes assured me, be better than being shark bait.

No one inquired as to my will, anyway. The men just went on making plans while Circe stood grinning like a fat seagull who'd gotten away with a prime oyster. When they tired of talking, they summoned a litter and placed my cage upon it.

"I shall deliver her to her new home," Aëetes offered agreeably. He was the youngest and least renowned of them, and this had been his idea. If he hadn't offered, he would have been ordered, and Aëetes, much like Circe, hated being ordered around.

"Brother," Circe turned her turbulent gaze on Aëetes, "let

me come along for the ride. I should like to see Scylla's new home for myself," she cajoled with a sneer.

Aëetes let out a snap of laughter and shook his head. "No, sister. After the strain you've been through today, I wouldn't want you to weary yourself on the journey. Rest up, Circe. Perhaps Scylla will invite you for tea once she's settled in. Though I rather doubt it." He smirked at his sister.

And then we were off, Aëetes seated in the front holding the sea horses' reins, me in the back, clutching the bars of my cage. We rode in silence for a time, passing through my father's kingdom, and I watched the familiar landscape of my youth pass by for the last time. I knew the moment we crossed out of my father's territory. It grew colder, and the magic changed. These uncharted waters were darker, less hospitable, answered only to Poseidon's might.

Aëetes stopped at the border for a moment, though I could not be sure whether to get his bearings or let me get mine. He turned around and gave me a sad, slow smile. He had the same dark, lanky hair and sallow skin as Circe, though it served him better as a man than it did her. The same beguiling gleam in his eyes, too, though his eyes, wild as they were, seemed kinder.

"I had hoped you would best my sister today, Scylla," he said softly.

I let out a little gasp. Had Aëetes known of Circe's plan and done nothing to stop her? Why hadn't he spoken up for me?

"Oh, don't look at me like that." He clucked his tongue. "Circe does not share her wicked little schemes with me, and I had no vision I might have warned you about. It's only that I know my sister. She grows overbold with her spells and concoctions. It is as your father said. A nymph is better off smiling and looking pretty than she is thirsting for power. Circe won't be far behind you in earning herself a banishment. And she's far more deserving of it. Honestly, you would think Glaucus would have been thrilled to be rid of that absurd fishtail, anyway, absurd thing that it is." Aëetes gave a dismissive wave of his hand.

I had no words, and apparently, Aëetes required none of me. He tossed a roguish grin in my direction, then clucked his tongue, urging the seahorses on, farther into the untamed darkness of the deep sea. We did not speak again until we approached the narrows. The current here was swift, and the seahorses bucked and struggled against it. Trapped as I was in this cage, in this loathsome body, I feared the whole carriage might overturn. But Aëetes reined the creatures into submission, then swam around to the door of my cage.

"This is where I must leave you, sweet Scylla," he said, his angular face solemn.

"Will I ever see you again?" I asked, though what I meant was would I ever see home again.

Aëetes quirked his lip up and shrugged. "I cannot say what will become of you, Scylla." His eyes got a faraway look in them as if seeing some vision in the swirling currents. "Likely not. But my sister—" he dropped off. Then he gestured, the motion a mirror image of Circe's when she'd captured me, and the bars of my cage turned to kelp, whisked away on the powerful current.

"The current will carry you to the cave in the narrows. Or, if you let it, it will carry you to the breakers along the shore and make an end of you there on the rocks. The choice is yours. But my suggestion? Make a life for yourself, Scylla. The best one you can," Circe's brother said gently before bounding back into his carriage.

Then with a flick of the reins, Aëetes was gone.

I let the slipstream take me where it would. Drifting, I considered Aëetes's parting words. What vision had he seen in these swirling rapids? Would Circe and I meet again?

Revenge was already becoming the thing that sustained me. The thing I craved. It would be this desire for revenge that kept me alive for a long time.

The rapids grew more turbulent. I floundered, sputtering as the waves tossed me about, filling my nose with seawater, burning my throat with sand and silt. I was in the strait. The narrows that would be my new home.

I could have let the current take me farther. Could have let it dash me against the rocks until my grotesque body was beyond repair. The curse of immortality can be broken easily enough. Even Gods die. But I was a coward. I was not brave enough to put an end to my own suffering. When the current whisked me past the cave mouth, I extended my long purple tentacles and grabbed for the rocks. They were powerful, those new appendages of mine, and I used their suction to haul myself into the cave.

The cold dark confines of four walls in the desolate narrows is no place for a nymph. We are creatures of laughter and light, creatures of passion and play. I looked around. It was empty inside but for a few small, eyeless fish suspended in the dim recesses, peculiar bioluminescent things, which I swatted angrily away. One day, I vowed I would punish Circe for this banishment. I did not know how, or when, but I would do it.

For, if Aëetes's vision had been a true one, she and I were not quite through with one another yet.

❧ 7 ❧

I SKULKED AROUND MY CAVE UNTIL MY BELLY BEGAN TO rumble. I gnashed the pointed teeth of my many heads until my gums bled. The hunger was unlike any I had felt before, a burning desperate need to feed. There was no sustenance within the cave. I'd tried one of the peculiar little fish, but they were bony and acidic and had done nothing to sate me. I would have to venture out to find something to eat. Carefully fastening my tentacles to the cave walls, I poked my head out.

And I saw him.

Charybdis.

He emerged from a churning whirlpool across the strait. A behemoth, his shoulders were the width of five men across, his head was massive and eyeless, his enormous mouth studded with green mossy teeth, longer and sharper than any sword. He let out a roar and pounded the water with a fist like a massive hammer.

I was so startled that I nearly lost my grip. Righting myself before the current could carry me away, I crawled back into my hole. This Charybdis was a true monster. This was to be my only companion for eternity? I curled up on the cold stone floor and wept tears of ink from my human eyes while my other monstrous heads gnashed their teeth and wailed with hunger.

The sound of screaming roused me from my weeping many hours later. I crept to the mouth of the cave and peered outside. Charybdis must have slept, for there was no sign of his horrific whirlpool.

But I did spot the source of the screams.

A desperately flailing mermaid was caught in the current, and though she beat her tail wildly, she could not free herself from the trap of the tides. At first, I meant only to help the poor creature. When I stretched my purple tentacles out to snatch her from the strait, I intended to set her free in calmer waters. But when she looked at me with horror and revulsion in her eyes...when she slapped at me with her vile fishtail, so like Glaucus's, I lost all restraint.

"Do you know, I was once more fair and lovely than you?" I crooned, dangling her upside down by her tail so that she could see my true face. The face of a beautiful nymph.

"You— you are still— you are still fair," the mermaid stammered, trying to charm me as mermaids always do. As I once did, too.

I drew one of my monstrous heads around and snarled at her, revealing my sharp rows of teeth. The mermaid shrieked, and my stomach roared in response, a deep rumbling like an earthquake in my guts. My monstrous tongue darted out and caressed her cheek. So young, so tender, she would be so tasty.

I could not resist. I snapped her in two with my jaws. Then I devoured her, my many heads fighting one another over bites of tender mermaid morsels.

For a long time, this was the way of it. Charybdis would wreck ships, and I would snag the stragglers from the waves, living off his scraps for sustenance. If a ship ventured out of his reach, I would pilfer a handful for sailors from its deck.

I needed to survive, you see. Circe's curse was more than just a wretched body and banishment. She had given me all the voracious appetites of a monster, and the looks in the sailors' eyes, those wide, terrified ogling eyes... well, they only stoked the beast inside me. The beast I had become. I felt no guilt over gorging myself on their flesh when they looked at me like that.

Years passed, and nothing changed. Years where I felt nothing but rage and hunger. And then, one day, I heard a familiar voice carried on the wind, chanting an oddly familiar song.

Circe.

I hauled myself out of my cave and fixed my eyes on the nearby island. I could barely make out her form. She stood alone, clutching a handful of flowers. Circe, always with her damnable accursed flowers. But... she was crying. It seemed Aëetes had been right after all. Here stood his sister on the shores of a deserted island. Banished, like myself. There could be no other explanation. I felt no pity for the witch. Only fury and frustration that she was right there, so close, yet still out of my reach.

I schemed, and I plotted. But none of my plans came to fruition. Circe's island was too far away from the mouth of my cave. To try to reach it would be suicide. I still remembered that mermaid, struggling against the current with her powerful tail and strong arms. In this monstrous body, I wouldn't stand a chance. Even if I made it to shore without being smashed upon the rocks, what then? I recalled the waves lapping at my inert bulk on the sand by the tide pools the day I had been changed.

No, Circe would have to come to me.

I watched, and I waited. Circe was up to her old tricks

again and seemed to have improved upon them. In her boredom, she had taken to harassing every ship that landed upon her shores. Turning mortals into swine became a favorite pastime of hers. Sometimes she even turned them into lions, who prowled her island like ferocious sentinels. Why they didn't eat her alive, I can't say. I know I certainly would have. Just more of her witchcraft, I suppose.

Oh, how I fumed with bitter jealousy when Odysseus landed upon her banks, and she seduced him. Even a pallid, scrawny witch like Circe could find comfort in a man's arms, a hero's arms no less. Yes, he was mortal, but he was a companion to her while I was stranded here alone. I admit I cackled with glee when the great champion of the Trojan wars abandoned her to return to his wife, and she grew big with child, just as alone as I was.

I could tell you much and more about how Circe raised that half-feral mortal brat. How he screamed and lamented endlessly as a babe and could be quieted only by the sea. How, as a boy, he was stubborn and bucked against that iron will of hers. I could share all sorts of stories about the pair of them.

But I won't. It's not my place. Those are Circe's stories, not mine.

Instead, I shall tell you of Medea, niece to Circe, daughter of Aëetes. For it is her tale that interweaves with mine.

It is Medea who, in the end, saved me from myself.

8

HAD IT NOT BEEN BATHED IN THE GOLDEN GLOW OF HERA'S light, I would likely have paid any heed to the ship. Ships arrived on Circe's tiny island often enough, though more than a few did not again depart. But this ship was curious, and I had little enough to occupy my time. So, I watched.

I knew who she was the moment I saw her standing on the prow. I had heard tales of her from the mermaids, who'd I taken to torturing for news before consuming. With her waifish frame and flowing dark hair, those flashing dark eyes, this could only be the daughter of Aëetes. The girl was very young and far more beautiful than her father or aunt had ever been, but the resemblance was still uncanny. They all shared the same features, but in this one, they were softened.

Medea.

I thought, perhaps, the first kindly thoughts I'd conjured up in decades then. I remembered Aëetes. I recalled his quick wit and the way he'd saved me from certain death. The way he'd tried to undermine his sister's lies. And his parting words to me.

Make a life for yourself, Scylla, the best life you can.

Now, upon the shores of Circe's island stood his beautiful daughter. I did not know what had brought her and her lover, Jason, to Circe's island. It was only later that the tales of Medea's betrayal of her father and the murder of her brother made it to my ears. At the time, I only knew it took great magic on Circe's part to cleanse them of their sins. The fires roared, and the waters churned with boiling blood on the night she performed the ritual.

They did not linger long on that strange island where pigs and lions prowled. Once the cleansing was complete, they seemed in a hurry to depart. I skulked around the cave mouth, watching them say their goodbyes.

"If you must pass through the strait, be warned," Circe said in her breathy voice. "Danger lies on either side. On one side, Charybdis. He has been a monster so long there is no humanity left to him. He will smash your ship and kill you all. Across the channel, Scylla. A monster of my own making. Less dangerous, to be sure. She is a weak, pathetic thing. No fight in her. She subsists on the scraps Charybdis leaves behind. Do not misunderstand me. She is a danger. But guide your ship towards Scylla's lair, and there is a chance you will make it out alive."

My many monstrous heads began to snap their teeth in fury at Circe's words. A weak, pathetic thing? How dare she! She who had made me this, who had created the monster I was. I would show Circe. I would dash their ship against the walls of my cave. Tear their bodies limb from limb and savor them slowly. I would show Circe that I was not simply a scavenger of Charybdis' kills.

I, too, could be fearsome.

I slunk back into my cave, watching for Medea's ship to approach the narrows. When I saw the sleek shining vessel enter the channel, I rose to my full height, clinging with a single tentacle to the cave wall. I roared, with all my monstrous heads, the sound chasing waves to ripple out, tossing their vessel wildly. The glow of Hera had faded from the ship. It seemed their sins had been too great for that great Goddess to forgive. Without Hera's blessing, I could smash it to pieces. Destroy it. Massacre all on board, just as Charybdis would have done.

I was moving in for the kill when I saw Medea move to the prow, her beautiful golden-haired Argonaut standing tall and proud beside her. Fools, making easy targets of themselves. They were nearly within the grasp of my long snakelike tentacles, the ones with the crab claw pincers, when Medea spoke.

"SCYLLA," she cried. "I know you are no monster, Scylla, daughter of Craetis. Your mother has told me your tale of woe. Do you know, Scylla, that Aëetes loved you? He would have asked for your hand if it were not for my Aunt Circe's meddling. He could not stand against the Sun God, but he did what he could for you. Let our ship pass. In payment for the boon he granted you long ago, let our ship pass."

Medea stared straight into my eyes. She did not gaze in horror at my flailing tentacles or my salivating monster heads with their jagged teeth and grinding jaws. The daughter of Aëetes looked at me. And she saw me. Me. Not the monster I was, but the girl I had been. The girl who her father had loved enough to save from becoming shark bait.

All those long years, and I had never known. Had never guessed that Aëetes cared for me. Had thought he had only wanted to foil his sister's plan. My mind reeled with the thoughts of the life I could have had. Inky tears began to stream from my eyes. All my eyes. The waters turned indigo with decades of grief as I lowered my tentacles, dropping them with a splash. I drew back my sharp-toothed heads, though they fought me in this, with prey so near.

I let Medea's ship pass, unmolested.

I was about to crawl back into my cave, to mourn all I'd lost and loathe what I'd become when the whirlpool that was Charybdis's harbinger began to swirl across the channel.

"That was impressive, Scylla, daughter of Craetis." Charybdis's voice was a low gravelly grumble that took me so by surprise that I nearly relinquished my grip on the cave wall and was swept away.

"You speak?" I gasped.

"Of course, I speak," the monster that was Charybdis growled. His whirlpool swirled faster as the towering gray form of his trunk stretched towards me.

"You never spoke before," I sniveled sullenly, wiping at my ink-smeared cheeks with my tentacles.

"You gave me no reason to speak before. You were a monster. I was a monster. What need did either of us have to speak with one another?" Charybdis shrugged or rather made a motion that passed for a shrug when one's body was little more than a massive shapeless trunk of flesh. "But today, you showed me... you are something else entirely. And it moved me. So, today, I reveal what I truly am. Just another small God like you. Cast down and stranded in this forsaken trait. I am a monster, yes. But I also am a man."

Do not get your hopes up. We did not become lovers. The channel was such that we two could never touch. But from the day I let Jason and Medea escape unmolested, Charybdis and I became something I thought I would spend eternity without.

We became friends. We became our true selves once more.

Yes, we still had to snatch a few sailors from the decks of

ships. One cannot blame the lion when he devours the antelope.

Even we monsters must do what we must to survive.

❧ III ❧
HEART AND SOUL

❦ I ❦

THE BEGINNING

THE MEMORY HAUNTS ME THE WAY FOSSILIZED TRACES OF the sea remain in the barren desert. A recollection from long ago, before the Oracle, the marriage, the trials. I was barely more than a child. Yet, it is so crisp and clear that it's almost not a memory at all; instead, it is a sliver of my past, perfectly preserved.

It is the true beginning, though I did not know it at the time.

It was autumn, and the leaves were all aflame and gold burnished. We were in some village or another. We frequented many shrines in those days, so I can't recall the name, and it does not matter. It was a pretty, provincial little town with lovely courtyard gardens in the town center.

I sat on the lip of a well in one such garden, picking out notes on a lyre. It was a beautiful instrument inset with chips of tortoise shells and goat horn. It wasn't mine, and my sisters would have been wroth to discover me playing it. Both Amara and Phaedra had been trained with lyre, flute, tibia, and plectron for years. Not me, though. I was destined for something else. I ought not callous my delicate fingers with strings or my soft lips with a reed. My lessons were of a different sort.

Still, I had an ear for music, and even self-taught, I could coax a pretty melody from almost any instrument. So, when I could manage it, I would sneak away to some secret place with a borrowed lute. Just as I had done that day.

I am not sure what snagged my attention. I must've heard a snap of a branch or the scuff of a boot upon stone. My fingers ceased their movements across the strings. I looked up...

And there he was, perched atop the stone retaining wall.

He was the most exquisite yet terrifying creature I had ever laid eyes on. His mahogany hair was light and sleek, falling in tousled curls that brushed his shoulders. From those broad shoulders extended majestic downy white wings, half-folded behind him.

I sat frozen, lips slightly parted, eyes fixed on him. My gaze shifted to the bow he held drawn in his hands. It glittered in the light, intricately chiseled, golden, and notched with an arrow that gleamed red as blood.

And it was pointed straight at me.

"Please..." the word was little more than a breath as it left my lips. His eyes, the color of the heavens themselves, narrowed as our gazes connected.

I already knew I loved him at that moment. He had no need for a quiver of magic arrows tipped in the sweet poison of passion. I was already charmed. Further enchantment would have been a waste. He could have stood before me as a mere mortal, with none of the tricks of his Godhead up his sleeve, and still, I would have loved him. He could have even been the beast they later claimed he was. Still, I would have given myself to him.

For like calls to like. Heart calls to soul.

I moved not a muscle, only stared back at him, waiting for the arrow to strike me down. His bowstring twanged. My heart rose up into my throat.

But he faltered.

The arrow went wide. He missed the shot.

2

INTERLUDE

THE CERULEAN WAVES SWELLED UP TO THE GODDESS' slender calves, gentle as a kitten, tamed by Poseidon's command. Aphrodite reclined on the alabaster sands, her face tilted up towards the warm rays Helios' chariot bore across the sky. Her eyes were closed to slits, her lips slightly parted.

She sensed her son's arrival and knew something was wrong. She could tell by the energy that bled from him. Desperate. Uncontained. Unhinged. He was always a passionate boy, but this was somehow different.

"What's happened?" Aphrodite craned her neck around, her gaze falling on Eros, who stood behind her, rigid and taut as his own bowstring. "Is it done?" she pressed him.

Eros shook his head. A lock of fair hair matching in hue to her own fell across his brow. A boyish curl cutting across his bronze, unlined forehead. And though he was not a boy any longer, now a grown man and a God, at that moment, he looked like the petulant child she'd once held to her breast.

"Why not? It was a simple enough task?" Aphrodite gazed at him with wonder in her expression.

She hadn't asked for anything overly difficult. Even for

this small-minded infant of a boy-God ought to have been able to deliver. One arrow to the heart of one girl. That was all. How could he have failed her, the woman who had birthed him into this world from her own milky white loins, in this one small task?

"I couldn't do it," Eros muttered, his gaze breaking from hers and burying itself in the sand at his feet.

"Why, that's ridiculous. You take aim, and you fire. You've never seemed to have a problem with it before. In fact, I daresay it's the one thing you're good at."

Eros scowled, then sighed, fingering his bow. He shook his head again as if trying to clear something from it. "Not this girl. I couldn't do it, Mother. I tried."

Aphrodite felt the color rising in her cheeks as her immortal blood burned hotter with irritation. "You do understand, this girl has humiliated me in the eyes of Gods and mortals alike? That her likeness stands in temples where mine belongs? She *must* be punished."

The Goddess of beauty slammed her fist down in the sand, a spray of it shooting towards Eros, who watched it scatter at his feet.

"Mother." Eros looked up, meeting Aphrodite's gaze again. Something wild and anguished swam in his oceanic blue eyes, and there was a note in his voice that Aphrodite was quite sure she had never heard before. A mournful plea that made her skin crawl.

She knew she was going to hate the next words that fell from his lips before he even spoke them.

"I am in love with her."

3

THE GIRL WHO WAS A GODDESS

It was all so long ago. Who can it hurt to speak of it now? To tell my side of the story, not recant the version told a hundred thousand times by the others. The world has all but forgotten magic, and even the Gods have been forsaken, left to slip into oblivion. My Olympus crumbles. So, why should I not tell my own tale to a world that remembers us only as of the stuff of myths and legends?

I was a fourteen-year-old mortal girl, thrust up on a pedestal so high that I could never have hoped to remain there. Aphrodite was ancient, immortal... and a jealous whore. My father knew this, but he was a King and a self-serving, opportunistic one at that. If the story had gone his way, I'd be moldering in the ground while he licked Ambrosia off Aphrodite's fingers.

Did he really think he could get away with parading me, a mere Princess, a child, all around the Gods' creation decked out in divine trappings without incurring Aphrodite's wrath? Of course not. My father had ambitions. He had plans. He knew what he was doing.

The first time he made me stand upon that dais, I had not

even flowered yet. Clothed in a perfect replica of Aphrodite's robes, my breasts were no more than rosebuds, barely bloomed beneath the thin layers of gauzy fabric. Every man, woman, and child who laid eyes upon me could see that I was no great beauty to rival the Goddess. I looked like exactly what I was... a little girl playing dress-up, with kohl lining my eyes, trembling as I blinked out at a crowd of farmers and merchants who thronged around me as if I was a broodmare up for auction.

"See my daughter, Psyche!" my father shouted. "See the Princess of these lands! Come! Does she not rival even Aphrodite in her grace and beauty?"

What a ridiculous claim. But my father was a commanding man with a powerful presence, and these people were simple peasants. They saw a fine circlet upon my golden curls, and some elegant cloth draped over a fair enough looking girl. If a King told them she rivaled the beauty of Aphrodite, well then, so be it. They would not argue. The king's words were law in those days. To speak against the claim of a King over such a trifle was unheard of.

We repeated this charade over and over. At first, my sisters Amara and Phaedra only laughed at the folly of their gangly little sister being hailed as a Goddess. But as the years passed, I grew closer to this ideal of beauty that my father pretended me to be. Perhaps it was a self-fulfilling prophecy, but as my likeness to the Goddess grew, so too did my sisters' jealousy.

WHEN I WAS SIXTEEN, we sat at the table for dinner, and Amara tugged on my carefully plaited hair until she tore free small clumps of my honey blonde locks and held them in her hands. At lessons, she pinched my arms, leaving red half-moon crescents where her nails bit into my skin.

"Oh, I'm such a beauty. Oh, look at me," she mocked as she tortured me daily.

Phaedra was kinder, her jealousy a subtler thing. She would secretly sabotage my needlework and feign ignorance when the tutor railed at my ineptitude. Still, at times, she would quietly chastise Amara for her cruelty. Not often, though. Mostly, she watched Amara's mean-spirited transgressions, mute. I could see the envy in her eyes. She was loath to leap to my defense because, in truth, she felt just as Amara did.

They were only girls, and I, their younger sister, was a Goddess. And they hated me for it. My placement upon this great pedestal had robbed something from them both. My father's love. The attention and affection of the masses. I desired neither, but that did not matter to them.

I tolerated their abuse silently and stoically. I could have gone to my father. I believe he had all but convinced himself I truly was one of the immortals. He would have warned away Phaedra's subtle acts of torture. He certainly would have whipped Amara silly if I had let on that she had defiled my sacred body by marking it with her nails. But I did not tell him.

You are, perhaps, wondering why. Why suffer so in silence when an end could be made of it? I cannot really explain, except to say that I truly believed I deserved it in my naïve mind. Why had I been chosen when they, older and no less beautiful, in my eyes, had been passed over? What right had I to so much adoration while they stood aside and received none? In short, I felt unworthy. So I took the punishment I believed in my heart I deserved.

FINALLY, the day came when my father declared he would seek husbands for us all. He invited the wealthiest and most eligible princes in the lands to our hall. Father no doubt expected great matches of all three of us, for Amara and Phaedra were lovely in their own right. But surely their marriages would not be nearly so lucrative as my own. After all, he had chiseled from my young and untried flesh his very own deity. Just as no man could resist the Goddess Aphrodite, the same must be true of me now. He could broker a deal for a vast Kingdom and wealth beyond imagining with a girl such as myself.

What he did not plan for, had not considered, was that he had made me into a woman made of stone. He had carved me into an idol, a cold creature of the Temples who men would worship but never truly love.

And so the suitors came. They filed into the halls, one after another, to seek the hand of King Antiochos' daughters. He was unsurprised when the first suitor asked for the hand of Phaedra. She was, after all, the oldest. The king who claimed her was a provincial man who ruled a pastoral land. Phaedra was wide-hipped and docile; surely she would be quick to give him heirs and would fall easily into the role of obedient wife.

He could even rationalize the wedding of Amara. The king who asked for her hand was a frivolous sort, best known for his wild parties and outrageous diversions. What would he want with an idol made of stone when he could have my spritely sister buzzing around his palace with her quick wit and voracious appetite for amusements?

Imagine my father's surprise, though, when after both my sisters were wedded and shipped off to distant lands, no offers at all came for the hand of his crown jewel, his Psyche? Oh yes, Princes great and small still came to our halls as suitors, feasting and gazing upon my face and heaping compliments and treasures at my feet... but each, in turn, passed me over for another elsewhere.

It seemed no one longed to marry the strange girl with the distant blue-eyed gaze of Aphrodite, whose likeness now stood in her place in all the temples of the Great King Antiochos' land.

FATHER BLAMED me for my lack of a husband and for withholding the wealth my marriage promised him. He accused me of dishonoring the Gods somehow, angering them and bringing a Curse down upon myself. He was the sort of king who would never be held responsible for his own folly. There was always another at fault. It's unlikely that it ever once occurred to him that, perhaps, in giving his mortal daughter a place amongst the Pantheon, he and I together had invoked the ire of the displaced Goddess Aphrodite herself.

I did not know, then, that jealous Aphrodite had already had her hand in my life. But she did.

❧ 4 ❧

THE ORACLE'S TIDINGS

WE TRAVELED TO DELPHI AND SOUGHT THE WISDOM OF the Oracle. It was a long journey, and for me, it was a difficult one. My father was a hard man, and I was not in his good graces. He spared me no discomfort, save to ensure my now mythical beauty remained unmarred. We traveled at a punishing pace. He spoke only to chastise me for whatever misdeed I had committed to bring this upon myself. I took the admonishments silently and with a bowed head. It was my way, then. I was still young, and I knew nothing other than to honor and obey my father.

Finally, we drew to a stop. The mountains loomed around us, forming a bowl of sorts with the grand columns of the temple at its center.

"Come along," my father growled. He took my arm and yanked me roughly from the carriage.

Eyes downcast, we climbed the temple steps.

"Hello?" my father called, his voice echoing off the cold stone. An elderly man in thick robes appeared at his call.

"Do you come to seek the wisdom of the oracle?" he croaked.

"Why else would I come to this pisshole in the middle of nowhere?" my father grumbled, scowling at the man. I flushed at his words but should not have been surprised. He dishonored the Gods, so why not a holy man too?

The man said nothing, only nodded solemnly and indicated with a nod that we should follow. He led us down winding hallways lit by flickering candles when we finally arrived. I expected he would be the one to reveal my fortune, but when we reached a cavernous room set with an altar, he turned abruptly and left us alone there. My father fidgeted and paced. Seldom left waiting, he was terribly impatient. I stood demurely by, silent and still as ever. A perfect statue of a girl, as always.

WHO KNOWS how much time passed? Moments spent in anticipation always seem to stretch on and defy the boundaries of time. Slowly, though, the room grew oddly warm and bright. It was as if an early summer sun was ascending within the enclosed space. I felt a sweat break out upon my brow, and the light grew more and more piercing. When I raised my hand to shade my eyes, my father swatted it back down to my side. I blinked rapidly against the rising of the brightness, finally forced to seal them closed against it.

When my eyes opened again, the room had muted to a subdued radiance. And a God sat perched upon a dais. I had seen many carved sculptures of Apollo. Nearly as many as I had seen of myself. None of them did justice to the God in the flesh, though. How could they? Mortal hands carved the marble in the temples, flawed renderings of something immortal and beyond our comprehension. The being before us was the pure embodiment of divinity. All the light we could not see pressed into form.

A wreath of laurels was set upon his brow, and a beautiful

lyre rested at his side. His eyes gleamed in his strikingly handsome face, and he gazed down at us not with malevolence but with interest. He appeared almost boyish, but I felt a terrifying and ancient power belying that youthful visage.

"Do you come seeking prophecy?" Apollo asked, his voice at once sharp and slippery.

My father thrust his chin up almost defiantly as he addressed the God on the dais. "I seek the fortune of my daughter. Most beautiful in the land is she... and yet... no man speaks for her hand. I fear a curse lies upon her." He redirected his attention to me, a bitter scowl impressed upon his face.

"Are you certain that you wish to know the hand the fates have dealt for her? It is often not what we wish to hear, nor what we expect. Such knowledge can be a great burden, especially for one so young." Apollo spoke gravely, arching a golden brow, his amber eyes burning into my father. Strangely, he did not so much as glance at me. It was as if I were invisible to him.

"Yes, yes, whatever it is, it is. We must know." My father waved his hand in frustration, impatience and irritation barely concealed.

Apollo looked away for a moment as if listening to a voice heard only by him. Briefly, a hint of a smile played at his lips. But it was gone so quickly it might have been imagined, replaced by a stern expression and a deep sigh.

"Mortal, I do not relish giving such tidings as these," Apollo began.

My blood ran cold with his words, but I remained rigid, my face an expressionless mask, as always. I shifted my gaze to my father and saw a pallor creep into his face.

It would serve us both right, I thought, if all of his schemes came to ill.

"Wed, your beautiful daughter Psyche will." With the

Prophetic God's words, I could see hope and greed gleam again in my father's eyes once more. Until Apollo went on. "Alas, it will not be one of the princely suitors you have beckoned to your halls. No. This child is destined instead for the monster of the mountain... a fearful beast so hideous that just to gaze upon him could still the human heart. Never shall she see his face, for the horror would be too much for one such as her. Were she to look upon him, she would perish."

One might think I would have wept and torn my hair upon learning this news. After all, I was a girl of seventeen. When the word spread throughout the land that I, Psyche, the most beautiful of all women, must wed a monster, I am told many did just that. Even my father let out a keening wail that sounded like a woman's as we stood in that marble hall and heard the voice of prophecy. Though I suspect he did not grieve for his poor doomed daughter, but rather for himself and his well-laid plans, crumbled now to dust.

But I did not cry. I only stared at Apollo, who tolerantly gave King Antiochos a moment to compose himself.

"But why? How is it possible?" My father took me by both shoulders, shaking me roughly. "What did you do, Psyche? What did you do to bring this curse upon yourself?" he demanded.

I went along with your plans. I masqueraded as a Goddess. I spat in the face of Aphrodite, I thought, though I said not a word.

"She did nothing," Apollo clarified. "It is the hand of the Fates at work here."

The brave King Antiochus let out a strangled cry like a small child, as his dreams of wealth and fame vanished into the haze of the thick incense. "Is there nothing we can do?" he cried. "Are you certain this isn't some sort of mistake?"

I flinched at his childishness. Apollo, the God of Prophecy, had himself bestowed this fate upon me. I felt confident that he was mistaken. To suggest such was an insult. Just as being a girl who pretended to be the Goddess of Beauty was an insult. I deserved this punishment. This was what came of disrespecting the immortals.

Apollo's voice was louder when he spoke again. It was a boom that resounded through the room. "There is nothing. You must deliver Psyche to the foot of the tallest mountain in the East of your Kingdom. Today. Then you must leave her to her fate." The coldness in his tone sent a shiver through me. Apollo was utterly indifferent to the fate he had condemned me to.

My father opened his mouth as if he would protest further, but he did not have time. There was a great burst of light and heat. I shielded my eyes, and when I removed my hands from my face, Apollo was gone.

5

INTERLUDE

THE DOOR TO APHRODITE'S CHAMBERS FLUNG OPEN WITH A resounding bang. Reclining on a divan, the Goddess of Beauty froze, mother-of-pearl inlaid brush still poised mid-stroke in a coil of her hair.

Her eyes flicked to Apollo, who stood in the doorway with arms folded across his chest. Unrestrained irritation blazed in his eyes, like a whip about to crack. But Aphrodite had no fear of the Prophetic God's rage.

"Well?" She resumed brushing with long, languorous strokes.

"It is done," Apollo replied, his handsome face puckering like he'd just swallowed something bitter. "Though it pained me to be the bearer of such heartache to the poor creature. This is a cruel game you play, Aphrodite." His brow creased in an even deeper furrow of consternation.

"I never claimed to be kind," Aphrodite replied, raising one slender shoulder in an indifferent shrug.

She felt the unbridled hatred in her son's gaze from across the room. Eros stood glaring at her, his blue eyes frosted like chips of ice. "Mother, this is vile, even for you," he spat.

Aphrodite's eyes, akin to his own, went bright and hard as flecks of tourmaline as they cut to Eros. "I gave you one job. Shoot the wretch and punish her for usurping my glory. You failed. And now you claim you love the mortal? Fine. Have her. But it will be on my terms, as we agreed."

Eros flung his arms in the air. "To make the girl believe she's wed to a monster? To make her live in darkness, never to see the face of the man she's to marry?"

Aphrodite's disgusted look could curdle goat's milk as she spat at her son, "You brought this on yourself."

Apollo gave Eros a defeated shrug, and a muscle twitched in Aphrodite's jaw. It was bad enough her fool of a son was smitten by the mortal girl... "Are you on this brat's side too, now, Apollo?" she snapped. "I was a fool to spoil and coddle you the way I did, Eros. So I see it was my mistake in your upbringing that led to this... pathetic weakness in you. But you, too, Apollo? Come now. Surely you see the justice in what I am doing. You're half a brother to me. Father would see the justice."

Apollo inclined his head deferentially to Aphrodite. "I am not in a position to take sides. But I wish you had not dragged me into the sordid affair. Mark my words, Aphrodite; no good will come from this ploy of yours."

Aphrodite snorted and let out a bark of laughter, her full rosebud lips pulling away from bright white teeth. "Is that... a prophecy Apollo?"

With a sigh, Apollo held out his hands in capitulation. "I will have no more part in this, Aphrodite. I have played the role you asked me to, but here, I withdraw myself. Eros, you are on your own now."

Eros' gaze shifted between his mother and his half-uncle. "We will be happy together. You will see," he ground out between clenched teeth.

"I hope you're right," Apollo murmured before turning on his heel.

Aphrodite only rolled her eyes.

6

THE CASTLE ON THE MOUNTAIN

My father wasted no time. We did not return to our home to collect my belongings. I was given no chance to say farewell to anyone. What did it matter? My sisters hated me. I was the girl of stone. I had no friends or lovers. We set off for the mountainous lands of the west, straight from Delphi. King Antiochos barely spoke to me as we made our way towards the great mountain where I would meet my doom.

These were lands unfamiliar to me. Where the grounds around our castle were verdant fields nestled along a deep and winding river, these lands were all painted in hues of gray and brown, the horizon slashed with jagged peaks, imposing ravines curling away on the sides of the road. I willed the horses to suffer a misstep, send the carriage careening down one of the steep inclines. But my fate was not so easily swayed.

We traveled for so many days, I did not bother to count them. Until finally, just as evening fell, we reached the base of a mountain so tall its summit was lost amid the clouds. There we stopped.

"So it has come to this, daughter," King Antiochos said,

gazing not at me but at the towering peak before us. Never before was the awkward and strained quality of our relationship more evident. My father, the great king, standing beside me, a seventeen-year-old girl about to marry a monster. Yet, he could not come up with a single word of comfort. *So it has come to this*, was all that he could muster.

"So it has," I replied, equally incapable of finding affection to express to him. For I had never known affection. It was as foreign to me as these wild, mountainous lands so far from my home.

"The people will weep for you," he added.

I was not a contrary girl, but I nearly rolled my eyes. After three years of parading me around the countryside like a trick goat, this was the consolation he had for me. That the people would weep.

I turned away from him then. I could feel the tears welling hot behind my eyes, and I did not want him to see me cry. So instead, I began to walk, picking my way up the steep slope in my little satin slippers, feeling each jagged stone beneath my feet.

When I turned back to wave goodbye, King Antiochos was already gone.

I sat down upon the mountainside, my fine robes dragging in the dirt, and I wept at last. I was not made of stone, after all. I cried for my sisters, who could find no pity in their hearts for me, only envy. I cried for my father, who loved me not as a daughter but as a means to an end. Mostly, I wept for myself, sitting alone on this desolate mountain with a strange and terrible fate awaiting me.

IT SEEMED like a long time passed before I heard a soft voice whispering. I lifted my head, looking around, but saw no one.

I strained my ears, vaguely wondering if I had gone mad with grief. Then I heard it again.

"Don't cry, sweet child." The words were breathy and seemingly disembodied. The air suddenly smelled sweet with hyacinth, though no flowers grew on the desolate slopes. "I know your plight seems terrible, but perhaps it's not so bad as all that."

The air before me seemed to swirl, and suddenly, the diaphanous form of a winged man coalesced before my eyes.

"Who are you?" I whispered, wide-eyed with wonder.

"I am called Zephyr, the West Wind. And you, I assume, are the one called Psyche? I have heard much of your beauty. The tales, it would seem, were true." The man made of air had a warm and gentle smile.

I sighed, wiping my red-rimmed eyes with the back of my hand. "Well, what a surprise... you've heard about my beauty. My father's lies have dazzled even the Winds." My voice was harsher than I'd meant, underlined with bitterness. But I felt my beauty to be a curse. The very thing that had brought me here to the foot of this mountain.

Zephyr did not seem to take offense, though. He just smiled wistfully at me. "The burden you carry is great, child. Allow me to ease it. What you find when you reach this summit may not be quite the horror you believe lies in wait. Allow me to carry you to the top to face your fears. The monster we know is often less terrifying than the one we've yet to face."

I thought about this for a moment. It could have been a trick... the Gods were known for playing with mortals for their own amusement. But what fate could be worse than the one I was already facing? If the West Wind spirited me away, would it be so bad? Zephyr's nebulous face was kind, and oh, how my feet ached in the little pink slippers.

"Alright. I accept your offer."

I took a step towards him, and he drew me close, wrapping his arms around me. Then he unfurled his diaphanous wings. I gasped, clinging so tightly to his neck that my knuckles went white as he launched from the side of the mountain into the air.

And then we were soaring. Up and up we went until the air was thick with the mist of clouds embracing us. My eyes darted over the crags and deep cut fissures as he rose above them, landing on a green-swept plateau that spread as far as the eye could see.

"Good luck, Psyche," the Zephyr's voice was barely more than a breath. He did not even wait for me to get my bearings before he swept away, leaving only the clean scent of dew-drenched meadows in his wake.

"But wait! Where do I go from here?" I called after him, but there was no response.

Alone again, I took in my surroundings. In the wildest dreams of my youthful fancy, I could not have conjured up such a magnificent creation as the estate upon the mountain. Where the mountain paths and passes were rocky and desolate, the land at the pinnacle sprawled out as if enchanted. Verdant fields fell away in all directions. Surely, this was some magic of the Gods, for how could a mountaintop surrounded by barren, dusty land be such an expanse of lush, fertile valley?

A lithe blonde maiden with a pretty sun freckled face appeared as if by magic, walking towards me.

"Hello," I said as she approached. She did not answer, but a trace of a smile crossed her lips, and she beckoned me to follow.

What else could I do but trail behind her as we crossed the meadows? In the distance, a majestic palace loomed up ahead. Towers rose into a sky just darkening with a rose-gold twilight, the last dying rays of sun caressing marble arches and sculpted verandas.

I paused for a moment, emitting a little gasp as I took in the scene. The girl turned back around, still silent, urging me forward with a twist of her head. Again, I followed.

The gates of the palace flung open as we approached the portico, revealing a grand salon. More marble. Statues chiseled into marbles lined the space far too beautiful, it seemed to me, to have been rendered by a mortal hand. Finely cast vases full of flowers of every hue rested on pedestals that flanked archways leading deeper into the heart of the palace.

"What is this place?" I asked as we crossed the threshold into the sprawling room.

Still, the girl did not speak. The only sound was her slippered feet whispering softly on the pale floors that seemed to glow in the sunlight. We walked down a hall lined with arches. I took a few curious glances as we passed by, and each room was more dazzling than the next. It put my father's palace to shame.

Finally, she stopped and gestured for me to pass through an arch on the right. I crossed the threshold and entered a large bed-chamber. An expansive canopied bed was oriented in the center of the room, soft drapes of sheer fabric draped over the tall wooden post. The balcony doors were flung wide, gauzy curtains fluttering lazily on the sweet breeze perfumed with wildflowers and fresh mountain air.

When I turned around to question the silent girl further, she had disappeared. With little else to do, I curled up on the bed. The down seemed to be a cloud beneath me. The satin sheets pulled up around my chin were softer than any I'd ever felt before. I drifted off into the sweet dreamless sleep of the utterly exhausted.

✻ 7 ✻

ONE RULE

WHEN I WOKE UP, THE ROOM WAS DARK. NOT DARK LIKE an evening room with drawn curtains. It was a total, all-consuming blackness unlike any I had ever experienced. A darkness that had never felt the pinprick of stars or even a sickled sliver of moon.

"Psyche..." a deep and intoxicatingly sweet male voice pervaded through the sleepy haze in my mind.

"Who's there?" I whispered, clutching the silk sheets tight against my chest.

"Your fate. The one you shall wed," the voice continued. Somehow, the sound of it lulled me into a peculiar sense of calm. Though I remembered the oracle's words and knew this must be the monster, I found myself unafraid.

"I will give you everything you have ever desired," the voice went on, a quicksilver thing, ringing out in the room, first here, then there as if he was circling me like a predator. But if I was his prey, I would be an easy catch. The voice drew me in, which was certainly not what one would expect from a monster.

"I will give you fragrant gardens to walk in, crystal clear pools to bathe in... all the wealth in the world. You will truly be the Goddess you have always wanted to be when you are with me."

A small voice inside me protested; that was not my dream. I had never wanted to be a Goddess. I only wanted to be loved. I never longed to be an idol with men prostrate at my feet. That was my father's dream, not my own.

Before I could voice that sentiment, he went on, his tone suddenly harsh. "There is only one rule by which you must abide. One rule which you must never, ever, break... or you will be cast out, never to see me again." He, this monster I was to marry, breathed his words into my neck, and I trembled all over.

"What is the rule? I will do as you ask."

I was pliable as a girl. Always bending to the will of others, longing to please them. That was part of what started the whole trouble.

The monster I was to marry seemed pleased with my easy acquiescence to his demands and went on to explain. "You must never look upon my face. If you can live with that, I will show you magic you have never dreamed of."

I frowned, furrowing my brow, vaguely recalling that Apollo had said as much at Delphi. That explained the impenetrable darkness. Still, I spoke out, a rare thing for me. "But why can I not look upon you? Surely you are not so hideous as they say. You do not sound–"

He silenced me by bringing his mouth close to mine. He licked my lips with a warm, teasing tongue, then darted it into my mouth. I gasped, unsure of what to do. Should I pull away? This was a stranger, but he was soon to be my husband. But the kiss... my first... it was magical. My entire body vibrated with it. Were all kisses so sweet?

When he pulled away, he said, "Blame the fates for that. Fickle things that they are. Only promise that you won't betray me in this request."

Of course, I swore to obey the one commandment. Even if I were more willful, like my sisters, I could not have denied him. This monster, if that's what he was, had me in his thrall, wrapped up so tightly into the web of his seduction with his godly tricks that I would've sworn to virtually anything. To this day, I still taunt him about this, and I think somewhere deep down, I am still angry at him for it and always will be.

I was a mortal girl of seventeen. Was it necessary for him to use that godly power of manipulation on me? Did he really need to enchant my will away from me? Tangled in the throes of desire as I was, I could deny him nothing. And I recognized that my will was not my own. Perhaps if he had taken the time to let me learn to love him as a man loves a woman, nothing that came to follow would have happened. I would have come to trust him. I would have denied the call of my curiosity and distrust.

But then... he was a God. Gods aren't known for their patience. Gods do what they will. It is in their nature to use their powers to claim the things they want. Zeus is a prime example. But I stray. The essence is, whatever we do, we cannot change a man from his nature, nor a God. And so he entranced me with his powers, and I fell into his thrall on that very first night.

His fingers brushed my cheek, then my throat. In the darkness, each touch was unexpected. I didn't know where he would land next, and each caress sent shivers of mingled fear and excitement down my spine. My chest thrummed a rhythm so fast I feared it would break.

"I would wed you tonight. For it is fate that we wed, and why delay?"

"Yes," I breathed the word as if it was pulled from my throat.

I felt a hand clasp mine. I could tell it was not his, the man I was to marry. The bones were small and delicate. The silent girl, I suspected. She led me away from the bed. I felt the whisper of a parted curtain brushing my cheek, and when we passed beyond that veil, suddenly there was light again.

We were in a small room with a large bath inset into a multi-colored mosaic-tiled floor. The girl indicated I should remove my clothes with a gesture, and my cheeks flushed crimson. With the faintest tinge of a smile, she recognized my shyness for what it was and turned away from me.

This was my fate. There was no sense in denying it. This was what came from living a lie. But perhaps Zephyr had been right. It might not be so terrible as I had feared.

I slowly removed my filthy traveling clothes, letting them fall to the multi-hued tile floor, then stepped into the bath. The water was warm and sweetly scented. I felt the tension stored in my muscles since beginning the long trek, first to the Oracle and then to this mountain, melt away.

There was no chariot as there was when my sisters were given in matrimony. No friends and family gathered to shower us with fruit and nuts. The girl dropped scented herbs and petals into the bath, mouthing soundless words, which I assumed were the customary prayers, as she washed my body, then my hair.

When she finished, she indicated such with a gentle squeeze on my shoulders. I stepped from the bath, naked and exposed, but only for a moment. The girl gently lifted soft gauzy robes up my arms and wrapped them around my front. She pulled the material closed, securing it with a sash. Taking my hand, she led me out of the baths, down the long corridor, and into the unnatural blackness of the bed-chamber.

I stood stock-still, the sensory deprivation causing me to strain my ears for any sound, making my skin prickle beneath.

"So now you're mine." Soft lips pressed against the sensitive skin behind my ear as he whispered the words. I nearly jumped out of my skin, but he steadied me, placing his hands on my shoulders and drawing me to him.

I could feel the strength of his desire pressed against my backside, and I shivered in anticipation and fear. My mother warned me a little about what to expect on my wedding night. When a man claims you as his bride.

This was no man. This was a monster. Or so Apollo had claimed.

"Pure as unpicked fruit," he whispered, and I turned my head, attempting to follow the sound of his voice. His presence surrounded me, the trail of his voice making me dizzy.

His fingers grazed my cheek, and I tilted into his touch. But he fled as soon as I felt him, only to pop up in another place. Little touches teased me. A thumb on the soft skin of my wrist, and I sighed at the caress. His fingers pulled on the lobe of my ear, and I whimpered at the unexpected contact.

His lips pressed firmly against my own, and I gasped when his tongue glided between their seam, parting them for his entrance. His tongue was thorough in its examination, exploring my mouth and inviting me to do the same.

My hands rose of their own accord but stopped away from his body, afraid to displease my new husband.

"You may touch me, Psyche," he whispered against my mouth, and my hands touched my husband for the first time. He had muscles sculpted like marble and skin as smooth as silk. *How could this man be a beast?*

His hands found the sash to my robe, and I stiffened when he pulled the satin away, allowing the gauzy material to part and slide from my shoulders.

Cool air enveloped my skin before hot air surrounded it.

"Ahhh," I cried out when his mouth latched onto my breast. The sensation was indescribable. Never had I imagined such pleasures were possible. His tongue caressed my nipple while his lips manipulated the taut flesh between his lips.

A hand glided down my side, and I writhed underneath his teasing touch.

"It pleases me, wife, to hear you whimper so," he said, and I whimpered again, contentment untold to have made my new husband happy.

"Husband," I gasped as his mouth suckled and nipped between my breasts before taking the other into his care.

I arched into him, already aching for more, but suddenly he was gone, and I stumbled on my feet.

"Husband?"

"Hmmm?"

The sound came from behind me, and I twisted on the spot, unsteady in the dark.

"Look at you, wife. Already desperate for me to fill you."

"Yes," I agreed, nodding, though I knew he couldn't see me.

His hand cupped my mound, and I cried out in surprise. His fingers dipped into my center, and my knees went weak. I threw out my arms, needing support, and they landed on a firm chest and broad shoulders.

"You're dripping wet. I want to feel you squirm underneath me."

"Yes, husband," I gasped. I dug my fingers into his flesh to stay on my feet. His presence was all-consuming; the fire pouring from my core was eating me alive.

He stepped away from me again. I cried out at the loss.

"So needy," he crooned.

His mouth landed on my belly, his hair tickling my

breasts.

"Yes," I cried out, more from euphoria than surprise. His fingers parted my core and pierced my deepest center. My knees gave out completely.

In one fell swoop, he had me in his arms, and I screamed out in terror and awe as he carried me across the room.

His knee came to rest on a mattress, and he lowered me to the bed, gentle despite the power held tightly contained in his body.

My husband spread my legs, and I shuddered when his tongue slid against my ankle.

"I will take you like a husband takes a wife and claim you for all the world to see," he said, and the rumble of his voice against my inner knee sent shivers up my spine. I was lost to him. Lost to the feeling of his hands parting my thighs. To the sensation of his breath against the curls between my legs.

Just like he wanted, I squirmed with madness when his tongue pushed inside me, and he used his massive thumbs to enter my canal.

"Husband!"

Rapture rippled down my limbs. My muscles shook and spasmed. My husband groaned against my sensitive flesh, nipping and biting as he worked his way over my hips. He stopped to suckle at my breasts before his lips latched onto my neck.

His fingers replaced his tongue between my legs, and I wished I could see his face. I wanted to watch as he took me for the first time. I wanted to see my ecstasy reflected in his eyes.

If this was what pleasure felt like, I understood why it was considered a sacrament between a man and his wife. If this was laying with a monster, I would have it no other way.

"You are mine," my husband growled into my ear. He

grasped my knee with his fingers, and while I was still lost to the bliss, he sunk his manhood into my core.

I cried out at the sensation, the pain piercing and sharp. But my husband did not give me a chance to suffer before lifting himself and doing it again.

Then again.

By the third time he sheathed his member in my folds, I was moaning in pleasure instead of pain.

The stretch of him was exquisite. With every stroke of his hips, he fanned the fire already building inside me again. He pinned my arms above my head, and I quivered at the pull of it, how it drew my body. He used me for his pleasure, and it pleased me to worship him.

They claimed he was a monster. But to me, on that first night, he was a God. If I were a smarter girl, I would have unraveled the mystery on that very night. But I was too lost in him and his touch to consider prophecy.

"Such a good wife," he praised me, and I keened at the knowledge that I had made him proud. Lewd sounds slipped from his lips. The slap of skin on skin echoed in the darkness.

Though I tried to be a proper wife for him, I couldn't contain my need, and soon my hips were rising to meet his. Against my will or wishes, my other leg lifted to wrap around his waist. It pleased him, if his grunt and quickened pace were anything to go by.

My stomach roiled, and my hips convulsed, and as was his wish, I was squirming underneath him. Praying to him, my God, that he offers me release again.

"Please, Husband, please," I begged, and at the snap of his hips and the power of his body, I broke into a thousand pieces.

He growled into my ear as his body stiffened above me. At first, I was afraid I'd hurt him in my inexperience and desire.

Then I felt his member fill me with his seed, and I realized I hadn't hurt him at all.

I had fulfilled my duty.

I was a wife.

We were fated. We were one.

8

INTERLUDE

APHRODITE TRACED A PLUMP DATE ALONG HER SENSUAL lips, then popped it in her mouth. "I hope you're finding your new arrangement to your liking. How is your new *mortal* bride?" She spat the word *mortal* as if it were poison.

Eros scowled, and Aphrodite smirked. "She is perfect in every way. We are happy. Happier than any man and wife have ever been. You failed, Mother. You will not ruin us, and you can not tear us apart with your wicked, jealous games."

Aphrodite fumed, her creamy white face painted with a deep scowl. "The arrogant wench only loves you for your Godhead," she growled.

Eros laughed bitterly, dragging a hand across his jaw in frustration. "She does not even know I'm a God, thanks to you. So tell me how that's even possible, Mother? No. I loved her at first sight, and she loves me even blind. The fates have spoken, Mother, why don't you relent and just let us be?"

Aphrodite waved a dismissive hand in the air. "She knows. I'm sure she must somehow. That is what she's longed for all along – immortality for herself. To supplant me as the Goddess of Beauty—"

Eros interrupted the diatribe with a sharp bark of laugh-ter. Then he shook his head, suddenly looking pensive. "I do not think that was the way of it. The girl hasn't a vain bone in her body. I think the statues were her father's idea, not hers."

Aphrodite stared at him, her jaw slack, eyes wide with disbelief. "Did you poke yourself with one of your own arrows, you fool? The girl is a trollop, a tramp. She's probably fucked half of Greece to earn her reputation."

"That is not true! She came to me pure!" Eros snarled, his lips curling back, revealing his straight what teeth.

Aphrodite was unphased. She went on, "You know, we can end this charade. It would be easy enough to send her back to her father, a ruined woman. That would be punishment enough for me. You would be free to carry on as you were before. You know, Eros, there are many fish in the sea—"

Eros sighed, weary of the debate. "I love her, Mother. I do not wish to ruin her or return her to her father. Why can't you understand that?"

The Goddess of Beauty snorted, pulling a pomegranate from the fruit bowl beside her throne. She peeled away the thick skin with her sharp nails, blood-red juices running down her hands.

"She will disappoint you, Eros. Wait and see. This match is a mistake. She is a mortal girl, and she has somehow pulled the wool over your eyes, but she will betray you in the end."

❧ 9 ❧

THE CALM BEFORE THE STORM

I SANK INTO SOMETHING LIKE CONTENTMENT, TO MY surprise, during my early days at the palace. My days became my nights. I had expected it would become difficult to adjust to this, but surprisingly, it was not.

I was always better suited for life in the shadows, despite the limelight my father subjected me to. There was a quiet stillness in my life that I had never before experienced. No crowds of worshippers. No elaborate rituals to maintain my beauty. No taunting sisters... at least, not yet.

I slept through the hazy heat of the afternoons and rose when the Helios' chariot was dipping down beneath the Western mountaintops. I would unplait my golden hair and brush the curls until they shone, dress in one of the many fine silks that graced my wardrobe, paint my face, and become a beauty my love would never see.

I spent my nights at my husband's side. Husband, that was what I called him, for he would no sooner divulge his full name than he would reveal his face. These were the rules. Another girl might have been troubled by them, but I was not. This was my fate, and I resigned myself to it. We hungered for one another. Yearned in a way that I could never have imagined. In bed in the dark, discovering one another with words and touch until Helios' chariot crossed the sky again. Then my husband would flee, and I would sleep away the day.

But it was more than just passion uniting us. Our words daily drew us closer together. I began to feel less frozen, less like a girl of stone. With him, I discovered myself.

"TELL ME OF YOUR MOTHER," he said one night as we lay in bed beside one another in the great canopied bed. My lips parted to speak, but I could not find the words. The night was unusually still. No breeze stirred the sultry air, the silence interrupted only by the crickets and tree frogs.

That quietude hovered between us for a long beat as I hesitated. Finally, I stammered out that I could not.

"My mother died when I was very young, along with my brother, the son and heir my father had so desperately wanted. If I close my eyes, I can remember small things, silly little things. She would hum while she braided my hair. She sang often. After she died, there was no more singing allowed in my father's halls."

"You may sing in my halls whenever your heart desires, Psyche." My husband drew me close to him, cupped my breasts in his hands, nuzzled my neck with his soft lips.

"I have never sung, Husband. I'm not even sure I could carry a tune if I wanted to." Girls made of marble did not sing.

His fingers moved in circles around my nipples, which puckered, erect with desire at his touch.

"I have heard you scream, my love. I know you have quite the set of lungs. I'm sure you'd make a fine singer."

I giggled. "And what of yours?" I asked.

"My what? My voice?"

Of course, I hadn't meant his voice. Though I had never heard him sing, his bright honeyed voice could only be lovely. Surely angels did not sing as beautifully as him. I pushed at his shoulder playfully. "Not your voice. Your mother."

I shifted closer, resting my head in the space between his neck and his shoulder where it fit so perfectly. Our bodies were made for one another.

"Oh... my mother." There was a sudden strained quality to his voice. "...Well... she is very beautiful,"—he ruffled my hair —"though not as striking as you."

I laughed. "Don't tease. You have never even seen me. We are always in darkness. I could be a ragged pock-marked thing." I swatted his hands away from my breasts, but he caught my arm and gently drew my fingers to his lips to kiss each one.

"I have touched every last bit of you, Psyche. I would know if you were pocked and ragged," he said with a chuckle, releasing my hand, brushing his lightly calloused fingers across my cheek.

His words touched a chord. Yes, he had touched every part of me. And I had touched him, too. And no part of him had ever felt monstrous as he was said to be. I reached out to trace the smooth skin of his perfectly aquiline nose. But as if he had read my mind, he was gone.

I sighed, returning to the previous topic. "Tell me more about your mother."

Why? Why did I want to hear tales of maternal love, of the tenderness with which she had raised him, of all the things that had and would never be a part of my life? Curiosity, I suppose. If he *was* a monster, and I was beginning to have my doubts, had he been one as a child, too? Or was it some curse that had struck later? Had he displeased the Gods and suffered a cursed?

"No. I will speak of her no more." His voice went colder than the north wind, rivaling Boreas' life-devouring breath, and I flinched at the sound of it. It was the angriest I'd ever heard him, and the bitter frigidity seemed to leak into the room.

Then he was beside me on the bed again, his fingers tracing along my collarbone. He became gentle once more, and the warmth returned to the room. "My mother and I are at odds, Psyche. I'd rather not let her take up space in my mind when I'm spending time with you."

How mercurial, how changeable this husband of mine was. I should have known then what he was. For weren't the Gods known for their changeability?

I knew he had risen because I felt the shift beneath me with the absence of his weight. A moment later, his hands clasped mine, and he pulled me to my feet.

"I want to show you something," he whispered. "But you'll need to trust me. Do you?"

My heart beat picked up. Was he, at last, going to reveal himself to me? Let me set eyes on his face and body? Did I want him to? What if it was true and to gaze on him really would mean my death? I swallowed hard, braced myself, and said, "You are my husband. It is my duty to do what you will me to," I answered finally.

He clicked his tongue. There was playfulness in his voice. "That is not what I asked. I asked if you trust me."

I didn't answer right away. I mulled his question over, turning it about in my mind until I finally decided, "I do indeed, Husband."

I felt the brush of his hand across my cheek, rustling my hair, and then something else... The softest silk. A blindfold. He tied it carefully, covering my eyes. In the pitch black of the bedroom, it changed nothing.

"Come."

He guided me. I didn't know where we were going, but soon I felt a rush of wind caress my face. The scents of narcissus and hyacinth tickled my nose. Familiar aromas that made a sudden pang of homesickness take me into its grip. Though little love was lost between my family and me, the scents were so reminiscent of my father's gardens. They brought my mind back in time to when I was just a girl, not yet playing at being a Goddess, not yet a pawn in the game of the fates.

"Are you alright?" Concern rows in my husband's voice. How did he know? How could he always read my emotions like that?

I cleared my throat and shook my head to dislodge the cobwebs of memories. "I'm fine. Where are we?"

I had become accustomed to darkness and blindness - but only within his halls. To venture beyond them, out into the world without my sight, was something new. It set my heart racing as fast as humming bird's, frantic beats against my ribcage, anxiety honing my other senses as I strained to compensate for my lack of vision.

"The summer gardens."

Summer! Had time really moved so quickly? I had arrived on the first budding breaths of spring, and now the summer gardens were in bloom?

His hands pressed lightly upon my shoulders, and I understood the wordless indication that I should sit. I lowered myself to my knees, feeling the soft grass tickle the exposed skin of my calves.

"I want to teach you to experience the world as I do." His words were an airy breath against my ear, and his large, strong hands encircled my fingers. "Just listen," he whispered.

And I did. I listened, and I learned.

I came to know things I never imagined possible with him in the summer garden. My husband taught me to listen, listen so closely that I could hear the chatter of the creatures great and small, the soft, wistful breath of every flower. It was like learning a thousand new languages, discovering a whole new world that had existed just beneath the veil of our own.

These were things most mortals would never come to know. They did not live in silence as we did. They did not live in darkness. Our fingers saw what our eye could not, in one another and in our world. One day soon, these things I learned would become my weapons against the worst blow fate could ever inflict on me.

On that day, together in the garden, we were happy.

But it was not to last.

✿ 10 ✿

SEEDS OF DOUBT

WHY DO WE LET OTHERS SABOTAGE OUR HAPPINESS? HOW is it we do not see their jealousy and their pettiness for what they are before we let them poison our hearts and homes? Is it really so much easier to believe the voice that whispers venom than to see the sweetness that surrounds us?

In my case, it was.

We had been married nearly six months when the silent girl, who I had by then come to know as Larenda, knocked upon my door and handed me a letter. She held it out in her small hand, her brow furrowed as if she already knew the tidings it bore would wreck our happy home. And she likely did. But the story of the girl is one for another day. Larenda's story is not mine to tell. Her silence is hers alone to break.

Faintly bemused, I thanked her, accepted the missive, broke the wax seal, and read the words. It was a letter signed by my sister Amara. She wished to visit with Phaedra, no doubt to gloat over my poor pathetic existence sequestered away on top of a mountain.

I giggled a little to myself. How surprised Amara would be to find that I lived in contentment here, that no matter how gruesome my husband was said to be, he was kind, even-tempered, and a lover beyond compare. That we had luxuries that she and my sister could only dream of having with the little princes they'd been so thrilled to steal from me.

I wore a smug smile as I penned my reply. I would show my sisters that after all, I had done all right. I was no longer the girl wrought from marble, the frightened, frigid, delicate child who might shatter like thin ice with their taunts. I was a new Psyche now, and I would bring them here to see.

"Larenda, friend, would you deliver my reply to my sister Amara?" I asked, holding the missive out to her. The sun had just set, and my husband would, I knew, be waiting.

She did not reach out to take the letter from my hand. Instead, she gave me an odd, uncertain look. If only I would have heeded the warning in her eyes! If only she could have spoken her concerns to me. So much heartache would have been spared.

But Larenda is what she is, just as I am what I am.

She did not speak, and I did not acknowledge her furrowed brow and down turned lips. Instead, I reached out, took her tiny hand in mine, and pressed the letter into it. And then I was gone, skipping down the palace corridors to lose myself to the blackness and the thrill of my faceless husband's embrace.

MY SISTERS SENT NO REPLY. They simply appeared one day at the gates of the castle, wearing looks of awe on their faces as they took in the majesty of my domain. It was autumn by then. The forests and meadows surrounding our palace had shed their summer greens and were resplendent with scarlet, ochre, and gold. A dazzling world for them to behold.

I smiled shyly and invited them in. It had been so long since I'd seen Amara and Phaedra, with them both having gone off to their husband's kingdoms and me being trapped upon this mountain. I thought perhaps now, now that we were all women grown, things would change between us. Now that I was no longer the marble girl on the pedestal, I hoped we could start over as sisters and perhaps even as friends.

I was a vain fool. I invited the vipers in through my front door, believing them harmless. But they were ready to strike, the venom of jealousy hot on their forked tongues.

Not knowing the trap I was about to be led into, I ushered them up to the highest parapet to watch the sun go down. They were silent. For the first time ever, it seemed they had no words. Struck as dumb as Larenda by the magic of this place.

Until the following day.

We sat at the table in the grand hall, devouring the delicious tiganites; small pancakes with walnuts drizzled with honey. Amara chewed her mouthful of food, swallowed, and gave me a sly look. It reminded me so much of when we were young that a shiver crawled up my spine, and I shuddered.

"So, is he truly a beast? Is he horrible? Does he beat you and mock you? Does he... bite?" Amara twittered out a laugh as if she meant her words as a joke. But there was a hardness in her eyes that I recognized. I had a sinking feeling it would make her day to learn the rumors were true—that he truly was a vicious monster.

I shook my head fervently. "Oh no, Amara... he is so kind to me! If only you knew! He is sweet and gentle as can be."

Amara scoffed. "He is a beast and a monster. Sister, you have always been a little fool, always doing as you're told, never questioning anything. 'Here, Psyche, stand upon this dais... Here, Psyche climb this Gods forsaken mountain in the middle of nowhere. Here, Psyche, marry this beast who hides his true face from you beneath a veil of night.' Did you not stop to think, sister, that this beast likely hides more than his

KATE SEGER

face? That he is lulling you into false security with all of these kindnesses while you blithely follow orders?"

In the wake of her words, I felt my triumph dwindle. I was once again that stupid little girl who followed every order, catered to every plan, never once protesting. Dimly, I heard Phaedra cluck her tongue in mock sympathy. Suddenly, I felt cold and ill.

"Sister, you don't look well," she said. Her concern was a false saccharine thing that made my stomach twist further.

"I think I need a rest. The heat is a bit oppressive today..." I began lamely, hating the tremor in my voice. I moved to rise, but Phaedra placed a lily-white hand on my arm and drew me back down into my seat.

I gazed at the sharp half-moon curves of her fingernails, remembering when she would pinch my arms at my father's table. My skin felt as if it were burning against her unwelcome touch, and I brushed her hand away.

"He will kill you, sister. You will not even see it coming, the knife in the darkness."

I blinked at Phaedra. "What? Why would he kill me?"

"Because he is a monster, as Apollo said. And that is what monsters do."

"How dare you?" I demanded. I was shaking, livid as I had never allowed myself to be before. This jealous witch who called herself sister dared try to sabotage my marriage? The first pure joy I had ever known in my pathetic existence.

"Psyche, Phaedra only wants to help..." Amara began lightly.

The black glower I turned on her silenced her at once. She twittered with nervous laughter, and I hated the sound, for it again reminded me of childhood. It was the same giggle she'd used when we were girls and she was afraid she had been caught doing something wrong.

"Get out." I kept my tone even, balled my fists at my sides so my sisters could not see how my hands shook.

They exchanged a glance with one another, then got to their feet, nearly synchronized, and all but fled my palace.

And I hoped never to see their scheming, envious faces again.

✢ II ✣

BY CANDLELIGHT

I MAY HAVE FELT THAT I HAD WON AT THE MOMENT AS MY sisters scurried back, chastened, to their castles. I had not. For I was still a stupid little girl in my heart... so easily influenced by others. Oh, how simple it had been for them to sow those seeds of doubt in my heart. And though I had driven Phaedra and Amara off, I could not dig up those doubts that they had planted. They grew, slowly, into tangled vines that seemed as if they would strangle me.

After all, surely after this time had passed, surely since we had grown so close, my love might now show me his face? Had I not proved that my love for him was true? No physical horror could be enough to drive me from his side. So why must we maintain this veil if he did not have some nefarious plan? If he did not intend to commit some horror when I was lulled into complacency and blind to it?

"My love," I said that evening in the post-coital bliss when our limbs and sheets tangled amongst one another. "Can I not look upon your face at last?"

I felt him tense. His body went rigid beneath my touch.

"Psyche, you can ask me for anything. I will lasso the

92

moon for you. But do not ask me for that." His voice was soft but firm, brooking no room for argument.

He touched me in the darkness, his fingers coming to rest lightly on my thigh. It sent a thrill through me, but I pushed the sensation away, and his hand too.

"Psyche, don't be like that," he murmured.

I only rolled over and faced away. In my womb, the secret I kept, the new life we'd created, stirred, and fear shot through me. Would this child be a monster too? Would he kill me, as my sisters predicted, ending this spark of life before it ever had a chance to embrace the flame of life?

My husband's sigh caressed my neck. I ignored it and closed my eyes. For a long time, I laid like that, awake but perfectly still. Waiting. Waiting for the steady breathing, indicating he was deep in slumber. I had to know the truth. I could go on like this no longer. Not with another life growing inside me. A life that had to be protected at all costs.

I rose, crossing the darkened room by memory, making my way to the bath chamber. There, a candle always burned, lest I need to relieve myself in the night. I wrapped my fingers around the white wax shape and, cupping my hands around the flame, walked back into the bed-chamber.

His back was to me, smooth musculature gleaming bronze in the muted light created by my candle. I crossed to the other side of the bed, got down on my hands and knees, and then I raised the candle, letting its light dance over his face.

I was prepared for anything. Any horror of this world or another that might lie in our bed illuminated by my betrayal. I gazed at him in the lamplight... and oh, I was not prepared for what I saw.

There was no monster in my bed, neither was there a man. His divinity coursed through him like a golden filament. His body was arranged in the careless repose of his slumber, naked, perfectly sculpted. And his face... boyish, radiant, emanating its own light to rival my small flame. It was a face I would know anywhere. Like myself, his likeness was wrought in marble and bronze, erected in temples all the world over. The face of a God. A God who had once, long ago, stood before me with an arrow poised to strike me down. Yet, he had missed.

"Eros..." I whispered hoarsely. For now, I knew beyond a doubt who this golden and lithely muscled deity I shared a marriage bed with was. Eros. Son of Ares, the fierce and violent God of War, and even more terrifying to me... Aphrodite, the jealous, vengeful Goddess of Beauty, whose place I had usurped in temples and halls throughout the land.

My heart began to pound as if it would batter straight through my ribcage, and my hands began to shake. I could not stop them from trembling. They shook so violently that, as I drew the candle away to douse it, several droplets of hot wax dripped down the taper, landing on his skin. I watched it happen in slow motion, my mouth forming an o of horror, a silent scream. I had defied not only my husband... but the very Gods themselves, including the Goddess whose retribution I feared more than anything else in the world.

Eros' eyes flew open as the wax touched his flesh. They were the bright blue of a cloudless spring day at high noon, shot through with silver sparks. At first, he simply looked bemused as he brushed at the spots on his bare chest where the wax had fallen.

Then our gazes locked. I saw it all in that look. The stinging hurt of betrayal, the pure Godhead of fury, and a profound, heartbreaking loss.

"Oh, Psyche. You foolish mortal girl. Could you not trust me? Did I not give you everything you ever asked for, everything you desired? What have you done?"

He leaped from the bed, pushing me roughly aside. The

candle went flying, hot wax splattering onto the white silk sheets still damp from our lovemaking.

"Husband, wait!" I cried, but he was already running, fleeing from the room with inhumane speed. I heard the candle lying on the cold marble floor sizzle once, then go out. Blackness overtook our bed-chamber once more.

I took off after him, tears streaming from my eyes, clumsy in my confusion and terror, unable to find my way down the winding halls in the darkness. I cursed myself for letting the candle go out. With it, maybe I would have had a chance of catching him, I told myself.

In truth, I never could have caught him unless he wished me to. He was a God with all the tricks of immortality at his disposal to escape my pursuit. I was just a girl, barefoot and clad only in my night shift.

Still, I ran after him, out of the darkened palace, into the star splashed midnight fields.

12

INTERLUDE

Eros flung the door to Aphrodite's chamber wide. The Goddess of Beauty started, dropping her hands from her weaving and cutting her eyes to where her son stood, nude, with tousled sleep hair and unmistakable anguish in his eyes.

"What has happened?" she breathed. She had not seen him look distraught like this since that day upon the beach when he'd broken the news that he'd missed his shot. That Psyche's punishment has not been enacted.

"You were right." His voice was dull, emotionless as if all feeling had been leached from him.

Aphrodite bit her lip to stop the grin that threatened to expose itself from crossing her lips. She tried to muster her most sympathetic expression as she got to her feet and crossed the room to wrap her slender arms around her son.

"Oh, my poor boy. I'm so sorry." She swallowed her 'I told you so' and nearly choked on it. "Tell me all about it." She could only hope her gleeful curiosity did not come through in her words.

Eros sighed and extricated himself from his mother's

embrace, collapsing onto a settee. He hung his head and buried his face in his hands.

"I thought she trusted me. I did everything for her. I gave her everything. And yet she betrayed me." His confusion was palpable in his voice, which was thick, dull, nothing like the Eros who Aphrodite knew. She experienced a moment of alarm. In all the ages since his birth, she had never sensed such distress in him before.

"Oh, sweetling. I warned this would happen. Psyche is a mortal. She was never meant for one such as you," she said, and this time her sympathy was true. Much as she loathed the girl, she did not enjoy watching her son hurt.

"But... I loved her," Eros whispered, a single tear tracing down his cheek.

A thought appeared in Aphrodite's head. A cruel trick, perhaps. But one that might brighten her son's spirits, or, if not, at least allow her a little fun.

"Perhaps all is not lost, Eros. Maybe we can give Psyche another chance to prove her worthiness. An opportunity for redemption."

Eros raised his head and gazed at his mother with narrowed eyes. "What exactly do you have in mind?"

❧ 13 ❧

THE SEARCH

I DO NOT KNOW HOW LONG I WALKED OR WHAT I HOPED to find. Not Eros, of course. Surely he was back in Olympus at Aphrodite's knee, telling the tale of my betrayal as she nodded and said, "I told you so... this is what happens when Gods mix with mortals, my son. When has it ever ended well?"

If I hoped to traverse back down the mountain that I had scaled when I had arrived, that too was impossible. The path was blocked to me. Some trick of divinity, whose I could only guess, made the landscape strange and foreign. Try as I might, I could not run home to my father's halls in disgrace even if I wanted to.

After some time wandering, though, I found myself beside a swift-flowing river. I was damp with sweat, my muscles aching, feet sore. I laid down upon the grass, breathing the sweet scent of the last wildflowers of fall. Like me, they were weak, wilting.

As I lie there, I heard a sound. It was high and sweet, a breathy melody, a piped forest serenade of reed and breeze. Soft at first, but growing into an elegant crescendo. I rubbed at my face with the filthy hem of my dress, trying to wipe away my tears and clear my vision as I looked off towards the forest where the sound was emanating from.

And then I saw him.

I knew him for a God immediately. He was small, his head coming up no higher than my shoulder, and I was not a tall woman. His hindquarters were thick fur, and his hooves cleft, reminding me of the mountain goats who scaled the cliffs in my father's land. His face was human... well, mostly, with a ropey little beard and thick brows that he furrowed as he gazed at me from the edge of the woodlands. He was no great Olympian like Eros or his mother, but he was a God.

"Who are you?" I asked, clutching my shift tighter around me, suddenly feeling quite exposed and afraid. Recollections of Zeus and Leda flitted through my mind. Gods, even small Gods, were dangerous creatures who took what they wanted. *Was Eros such?* I wondered, but before I had time to muse on it, the goat-like God spoke.

"They call me Pan," he said matter-of-factly.

I wracked my brain. The name was vaguely familiar in the way of a half-remembered dream, but I couldn't place what this Pan held domain over.

"You know, God of shepherds, wild places... nature and rustic music." He drew his flute to his lips, and a flourishing little ditty erupted from it. "And who, my dear, are you?"

I gulped. I didn't dare lie to a God. But what if Aphrodite had sent him to punish me for my disobedience?

"My name is Psyche," I said.

This seemed to make no impression on him whatsoever, for he only asked me, "And why is that you weep, Psyche?"

"I have lost something, which I fear might never be found."

The half-smile he gave me was kind and grandfatherly. "Mayhaps I can help you find it?"

I studied him for a moment, unsure how much I dared give away. He might help me. Or he might call Aphrodite's wrath down upon my head. But what was I going to do? Wander the forests forever?

"The thing I seek is in Olympus," I explained, hoping he did not press me for more details.

Pan sucked his teeth and tugged at his beard. "I am an Old God, but I am also only a small God, half-forgotten by most," Pan said soberly. "I hold no sway in the courts of those great Olympians, with all their pomp and self-importance."

I would have despaired that he would be no help at all, but I noticed the playful smile toying at his lips.

"Of course, I do know one who might be able to aid you. She's not far from here..."

Hope bloomed inside me. So it was not a hopeless case. There is someone who might help me seek Eros and make my amends!

"Who? Where?" I breathed.

"A Temple of Demeter lies not far from here, west if you follow the river. Demeter might be able to help you reach the one you seek in Olympia."

I bounded to my feet. "Thank you. Oh, thank you, Pan. You may be a small God, but you are a great one to me!" I exclaimed.

He smiled and nodded his head, bringing his flute back to his lips. He raised his gnarled hands in a waving motion, ushering me towards the temple. I did not linger. I took off at a run, heading for Demeter's temple. I had to find Eros.

I FOUND the temple with ease once I knew which direction to head in. It sat on the west bank of the river, its columns rising against the muted hues of a gloaming sky. I stepped through the arched entryway and called out, "Hello?"

Only the echo of my own voice carried through the temple. It seemed abandoned, and the quiet set my nerves on edge. Hesitantly, I stepped forward into the main alcove where the towering statue of Demeter perched atop a podium, staring at me with lifeless marble eyes.

I fell to my knees before her, bowing my head and murmuring prayers and pleas to the stony rendering of the Goddess of the Harvest. I stayed prostrate for quite a long time as the shadows in the room lengthened, night replacing day outside. Finally, I rose with a sigh. If Demeter was here, she did not deign to recognize my desperate pleading.

"This is getting me nowhere," I said to the air. I looked around the room. Having been practically raised in temples, dragged from one to another by my father from the time I was old enough to stand upon a dais, I was more than familiar with how they were to be arrayed. As my eyes drifted around the temple, I realized how woefully disordered Demeter's shrine offerings were.

Unsure what my next step would be, I rose to my feet and brushed the seeds and dirt from my knees, clucking my tongue at the lazy Priestesses who had left the offerings strewn in such disarray. Idly, I began arranging them properly, polishing the scythes and lining them neatly at the foot of the altar, straightening the red and gold garlands strung about the room.

When I finished, I turned to go. Where? I did not know. But I would not relinquish my quest to find my lost love. I had already turned away from the altar and towards the arched double doors when I heard a soft sigh. A warm pale gold mist seemed to settle over the room, and the hairs on my neck prickled, much as they had in the presence of Apollo. And when I'd lain with Eros. *Fool!* I cursed myself again. Fool that I was, I had not recognized the sensation of divinity in him for what it was. Had I only done that, I would not be here right now.

But there was no sense cursing myself again now, for the hundredth time, so I slowly turned, lowering myself to my knees and bowing demurely.

"Great Goddess," I whispered, eyes downcast.

"So," she said, "you are the one Aphrodite rages so about." Her voice was gentle yet somehow chastening, like a mother speaking to a wayward child.

"Goddess, I never intended to anger Aphrodite. I wished only to gaze upon my husband's face." Demeter laughed at that, a rough sound like sheaves of wheat rubbing against one another.

"Oh, child. Surely you know the Goddess of Beauty was angry long before that!"

I had suspected as much for many long years. I had waited for Aphrodite's retribution most of my life, unaware that it was already upon me. I recalled the idols torn from their altars and replaced by my own likeness throughout my father's lands. I winced.

"She sent Eros to take care of you years ago. The joke in Olympus is that he carelessly stabbed himself with his own arrow when he was sent to take aim at you." Demeter's breathy laughter once again filled the room. When her chuckling diminished, she said, "Child, look at me."

I raised my eyes and met her gaze. Her eyes were deep amber and forest umber flecked with gold, shades of autumn moving throughout.

"Ah, yes. You are beautiful, but so very many mortals are. It's the soul in those green eyes of yours. I can see why he fell, though I can still hardly believe it. The mighty Eros, breaker of hearts, and a mortal girl."

I blushed crimson at her words. The child in my belly, the secret I had been keeping, the one I meant to tell Eros of after I saw his face, stirred. "I must find him again," I whispered, fierce in my resolution to make right what I had destroyed.

"I can summon her," Demeter said, sounding hesitant. Her face creased with uncertainty. "But be warned, what she has in store will be no easy task."

"Has in store?" I echoed.

Demeter nodded. "The Goddess seeks revenge yet. But in plotting your downfall, she has neglected to consider the chance of your success. If you play Aphrodite's game, there's a chance you can win back the God of Love's heart."

Hope bloomed within me like flowers unfurling beneath the first warm breath of spring. A chance! There was hope. But fear curdled the sweetness of the hope. To face Aphrodite would be to face my deepest fear, one that had haunted me most of my life.

But Eros... if there was even a shred of chance...

I steeled myself, set my jaw, and met Demeter's gaze. "I will do it."

Demeter's smile was wistful. "You are a brave soul, Psyche, daughter of Antiochus. Know the path will be difficult. Succeed, and you will win back what you've lost. Fail... and it will be the end of you."

Fear trilled through me. But without Eros, what was life? We had become two parts of the same whole, and without him, I felt nothing but emptiness.

"I will take my chances," I affirmed.

Demeter nodded. "Then close your eyes, child. The Goddess of Beauty awaits."

I took a deep breath, and I closed my eyes.

❧ 14 ❧

THE FIRST TRIAL

A COLD DEEPER THAN ANY I'D FELT BEFORE PASSED through me. It filled me, squeezing icy fingers around my heart, and I feared I'd made a grave mistake. Perhaps Demeter had lied, sending me to Hades instead of Aphrodite as payment for my sins.

It was a long time before I could bring myself to open my eyes. When I did, she stood before me. The Goddess of Beauty in the flesh.

"Do you know who I am?" she asked. Of course, I did. I had seen her likeness in hundreds of temples, only to be replaced with my own. I could hold no candle to the radiance Aphrodite emanated from her alabaster skin and radiant eyes that were so familiar... so like those of my husband.

But the beautiful horror of this angry Goddess was terrifyingly different from those cold carved statues. Here was a creature of fire and blood and wrath as well as unparalleled beauty. There was a cruel twist to her lips, impulsivity to her every movement that caused a deeply disquieting anxiety to bloom in my guts.

"You are Aphrodite," I whispered.

She laughed, and the sound was sharp as a blade, driven home into my breast and twisted.

"You are not quite so stupid as you look, mortal."

Aphrodite circled me like a ravenous wolf. Her movements were quick and graceful, sharp yet fluid. I twisted my head around to follow her as she seemed to float rather than walk over the marble floor.

"Did you know," she said, licking her viridian lips, showing her small white teeth, "that I sent my son to you to strike you down with an arrow long years ago? To shoot you with that fancy bow of his? Had he succeeded, you would have married a true monster. But perhaps this punishment is even more fitting. Perhaps his ineptitude worked to my advantage."

Her son. My husband. Eros. The love child of Aphrodite and Ares. So it was true then; he had taken aim at me in the gardens when I was just a child.

"He must have shot himself, the stupid ass, though he claims he did not. He claims he fell for your 'charms.'" Aphrodite bared her pearl-like teeth and went on. "When I told him he could not have you, we struck a deal. If he wed you blind and you did not betray his trust, he could keep you. His little mortal pet. Then roped Apollo into the whole mess, with the prophet on the mountain business. What does it matter, though? In the end, you failed the test." Aphrodite scowled, and despite her beauty, she looked fierce and terrible wearing the expression.

My stomach roiled, and I could feel the blood draining from my face. I knew instinctively that I must, above all else, keep the Demigod inside me a secret from the terrible wrath of Aphrodite.

"I would beg a boon," I breathed deep through my nose, willing nausea to pass, forcing my breathing to steady and become less ragged.

Aphrodite's laughter peeled out, echoing off the temple's marble walls, piercing and terrifying.

"You would ask something of me?" That laughter again, like a crack of thunder. "Not likely to be granted, but I will humor your whim, mortal. What is it you ask of me?"

I swallowed my fear, and when I spoke, my voice was steady and strong. "Give me another chance to prove my love for Eros, for your son. Demeter tells me you would offer me a trial to win back his love. I will do any task you demand. Anything at all."

Aphrodite's face changed at that moment. The rage dimmed, and cool calculation leaked into her bright-eyed gaze as she said, "Anything?"

I nodded. "Anything."

The Goddess of beauty brought her long slender fingers to her jaw, stroking it and tilting her head to one side, studying me. "Alright," she said slowly, drawing out the word. "But not offered as a boon to you. I do this purely for the enjoyment it will bring me to watch you fail."

"I will succeed. I swear it. My love is true. Eros is the other half of my whole. I would move heaven and earth to feel his touch once more."

Aphrodite snorted and rolled her eyes. "Yes, yes, noble as brave Achilles, you are. But remember what happened to him and his lover in the end." She threw me a vicious sharp-toothed smile, then extended her hand towards me. "Take my hand, and I'll reveal your first task."

It took every ounce of my resolve to reach out and grasp the hand of the Goddess.

But I did it. For Eros and for our child.

THE WORLD WENT dark around me. The blackness was deeper than even that of the chamber where Eros and I shared so many blind nights. Then, slowly, light began to trickle back into my vision. I found myself standing on a patch of dry earth that stretched for miles, with nothing to see in any direction but low scrub grass and thorned bushes.

Aphrodite released my hand, and the blood that seemed to have stilled in my veins began to pump once again. "Here, you will complete the first trial."

"And if I do this, you swear I will be able to see Eros once and make amends?"

Aphrodite's look went stormy. "This is the path to my son."

I realized then that whatever she had in store for me was more than this one task. To succeed, I would have to complete them all. Dread coiled inside me.

"What is the task?" I whispered.

She gestured at the ground. There, at my feet, sat a large pile of seeds of various shapes and sizes. "Sort them. No seed mixed with another that is not of its ilk. Succeed in this, and I shall grant your heart's desire."

I stared at the mound of seeds. There were thousands of them, and no two seemed alike. How was I ever to accomplish such an impossible task?

"But—" I began, but Aphrodite cut me off with a hiss.

"You brought this upon yourself. This is the task. You will succeed, or you will fail. I shall be back to inspect your work at sunset."

And before I could utter another word, she lifted her hands into the air, and she vanished.

The task seemed impossible. I sat upon the dusty red earth and wept bitter tears, taking a handful of the seeds and slipping them through my fingers. Aphrodite had been right, as had Eros, my beautiful betrayed lover, when they had called me a fool. I was a stupid mortal girl. What made me think I could fight the will of the Gods?

I cried until my tears ran dry. Then I stilled. I drew myself into that secret silent place Eros had taught me to find in the gardens. I peeled back the veil, and I listened to what the world around me, and my heart, were telling me. Yes, the task seemed hopeless. Yes, I seemed utterly alone. But was I? No, far from it. There was a breeze, but fickle, changeable. On it, small voices carried. Whispers of the earth and its creatures.

I did not know what I had done until the spell was cast. So often, that is the way of it. We cast small magics with our laughter and our tears. We bend the world with our will. Longing is a power in and of itself.

It started with one small creature, such a tiny thing. A black speck creeping up and out of a tiny sandy mound in the ground. My sisters would've stomped on it. Even I, not so long ago, in the days before the garden on the mountain, would have carelessly brushed it away from me. No longer, though.

I hunched down low, dropping onto my belly, my face pressed to the ground, and watched, wide-eyed. More ants emerged from their earthen pyramid. They formed a small army, a line of workers, making their way to the pile of seeds Aphrodite had made for me.

Working with the perfect choreography of nature, the ants began to sort the seeds.

My tears sprang anew, but this time, I wept with joy.

APHRODITE ARRIVED as promised when the crimson and indigo hues of the sunset banded the sky. She appeared in a flash of brilliant light, ever dramatic, that forced me to shield my eyes. I pulled my hand away just in time to see her eyes fall to the neatly arranged piles of seeds amassed at her feet. Her smug expression shifted rapidly, first to bafflement and then to ire.

"How can it be? It is impossible." She gasped, her eyes shifting from one neat pile of seeds to the next.

They were arranged around me in a perfect circle, and Aphrodite stalked in a ring around them three times in an attempt to find something amiss. To find even one seed out of place.

In the end, she had to concede the seeds were perfectly sorted.

"May I see him now?" I pleaded. I even went so far as to shift to my knees, prostrate before her in my desperation.

Aphrodite scoffed. "No. This was only the first step. Come with me."

She snatched up my hand, and again, the world around me was overwhelmed with darkness.

THE SECOND TRIAL

WE STOOD ATOP A LOW HILLOCK HILL BESIDE A SMALL POND with murky waters, overlooking a land of succulent greenery. The rams were covered in a thick, golden fleece that shone in the sun. Amid the scattered trees and bushes, two beasts battled, locking horns, stomping, and snorting as they charged one another with violent fervor.

I turned my head to Aphrodite. A small, sly smile played at her lips. "I wish to weave golden thread upon my loom. Alas, I have none. *You* will fetch me some."

I stared at her, my heart beating fast in my chest. To approach these furious creatures would surely be suicide. They were large as oxen, and the ire radiating off them was palpable even from up here at a distance.

"Be careful, though. I wouldn't want you to get hurt. I'll return when Selene rests at the apex of the sky." Again, the Goddess of Beauty made her exit in a puff of scarlet smoke.

Midnight. I had until midnight to procure the golden fleece for Aphrodite. I watched the rams butting heads with weary resignation, despair settling in my bones. I took a tentative step towards them, the brush rasping beneath my footfall. Their heads turned towards me immediately and lowered their heads as if to charge.

I backed up a step, and they returned to fighting with one another.

Surely, there must be another way, I thought.

I remembered my experience with the first trial. When I stilled myself and found my center and locked into the world around me, the answer had come of its own accord. I closed my eyes and cleared my thoughts, listening to the world around me. The trickle of the pond waters rippling, the low huff of the wind in the trees. And something out in the rattling of the reeds...

All things must come to rest in time. No anger is eternal. No passion can go unquenched forever. All creatures must put aside their rage and sleep, the reeds seemed to whisper.

What were they trying to tell me? That my rest would bring answers? I mulled the idea over, and then the reeds rattled again.

The brambles bite, and by the dark of night, you might gather what you need without a fight.

The light went off in my head, and jubilation sprang into my heart. The thorn bushes that surrounded the field! I could collect the fleece from the bushes that surrounded their battlefield. Sooner or later, the vicious creatures would have to call it a night and sleep.

The wait was long. I began to fear that the reeds had been wrong, that these beasts required no rest and would keep up their raging battle for time eternal. Selene's crescent arced through the night sky, and the time for Aphrodite's return was drawing nigh.

Then, just as I gave up hope, it happened. The rams both lowered their heads. With weary steps, they walked side by side as if the battle of the day had never happened. Together, they left the field.

I glanced up. I did not have much time. I scampered down the hill, approaching the brush that surrounded the field. The fleece was there, bright in the moonlight. Being careful not to prick myself upon the razor-sharp brambles, I picked the wool from the bushes until my arms were full. I was about the pluck the last handful when the sky flashed bright scarlet.

Aphrodite appeared in the center of the field. Surprise crossed her face as her eyes landed on me. It was clear she had not expected me to survive. Or at least, not to survive *and* be bearing an armful of the rams' golden fleece. She glanced at my hand, still extended towards one of the bushes.

"Why, that is cheating!" she exclaimed, color rising high in her pale cheeks.

I looked at her and calmly shook my head. "You never said how I was to procure the fleece. There were no stipulations, no rules," I countered.

Her eyes narrowed. If a look could kill, hers would have done me in. But it seemed even the great Goddess Aphrodite could not manage that feat.

"You think you are smart, but in succeeding in these tasks, you have only sealed your own fate," she growled.

"This time's a charm," her voice sliced like a hot knife, echoing in the void that surrounded me. "Your final task is at hand. Bring me a sliver of beauty from the Mistress of the Underworld. Or be banished there for eternity."

A little shiver started at my spine and coursing up to stiffen my neck. Persephone. Aphrodite's rival for the love of Adonis. Surely she, the spurned lover, would be unwilling to give so much as a shred of her beauty to her rival.

Yet another impossible task, but I had to try. I lifted my chin and forced a stiff smile. "For the love of Eros, I will do it."

The glint in Aphrodite's eye was dangerous, like an

unsheathed knife. "We shall see," she uttered, raising her hand to gesture at me before disappearing into the blood-red ether.

The world went dark. There was a sensation like falling from a great height. My guts coiled up into my throat, hitting me with a wave of nausea. I dropped my hands protectively to my stomach, shielding that place where life grew. And I waited.

❧ 16 ❦

INTERLUDE

"You sent her where?" Eros enunciated each word slowly as if he was speaking to a child, his eyes owl-wide with disbelief at what he was hearing. Hades? His mother had sent Psyche, the love of his life, to the Underworld? To beg a boom from Persephone?

"Well, she would have wound up there sooner or later, anyway. All mortals do. I merely... hastened the process." Aphrodite's voice flickered, nervous. She drummed her fingers on her thigh, realizing that she might, perhaps, have taken the game a bit too far.

"Mother! This is not what we agreed to!" Eros roared enough, his fury so intense that the very foundation of Mount Olympus itself seemed to shudder.

Aphrodite and her son locked gazes in a battle of wills that neither could ever win. Eros shared her headstrong nature, cut through with the steel of his father, Ares, the God of War. And he would not be cowed by his mother any longer.

"We will both go back down to Hades. We will find her. And we will bring her back." Each word was sharp as a knife, slicing at the air in Aphrodite's chambers.

"I will do no such thing," Aphrodite snapped, folding her arms across her chest with a languid motion.

Eros closed the distance between himself and Aphrodite in three long strides. The Goddess of Beauty had never before noticed how imposing her son was. Though his frame was slender and lithely muscled like her own, he had inherited his father's height, and he towered over her, his face etched with rage.

"It might not be so simple," Aphrodite muttered under her breath.

"What was that?" Eros' hands came down on her shoulders, giving her a shake that made Aphrodite's teeth rattle in her mouth.

She glared at him. Fear and fury fought to control her face. "I already paid the boatman," she explained.

Eros released her with a hard shove, sending her sprawling across the room and landing in a heap on the floor.

"I'm going to talk to Zeus. He will hear of what you've done. *You had no right!*"

"Wait! Don't—" But it was too late; Eros had already stormed out the door.

Aphrodite brooded. If Zeus involved himself, all of her plans would be ruined. Unless...

She sighed. She would have to deal with Psyche herself. Before her son and her father made it to the Underworld.

❧ 17 ❧

THE UNDERWORLD

THE BOATMAN SAT ACROSS FROM ME, DRIVING THE BOAT forward with a long wooden pole. A hood covered his face, revealing only absolute darkness and two glowing orbs where his eyes should have been. We moved down a wide and sluggish river, passing a land where all the color seemed drained. The reeds and grasses were wilted as if touched by hoarfrost, and as the boat went onward, all vegetation, all signs of life, crumbled, born away off upon a swift, chill wind that made me shudder. A sick feeling of dread uncoiled in my belly, long fingers racing up to strangle my heart.

"What is this place?" I choked the words out past the knot of fear lodged in my throat.

The boatman remained silent, but it did not matter. I already knew. The underworld, the domain of Hades. A realm from which mortals did not return, except those few legends, worshipped in songs, penned in verse. Great heroes, not weak, pathetic girls like me. I swallowed hard.

We crawled down the river. For how long, I do not know. With no sun or moon to mark the time, the world seemed at a standstill. Souls wandered on the banks of the river, but none paid any heed to my passing. They drifted, their attention turned inward, their surroundings ignored.

And then the boat turned towards a narrow dock, guiding the vessel toward it. When we reached it, he gestured for me to disembark.

"Can you tell me where to find Persephone?" I asked, my voice hoarse with fear.

One slow shake of his head told me he would be no help. He pointed towards the dock again. I clambered to my feet, the boat rocking beneath me, and stepped out.

I wandered. This part of the Underworld seemed entirely empty. There were no souls in sight, no one I could ask for aid. And then—a series of low growls. Deep and guttural, they made my hair stand on end. I stood frozen. It was an act of consummate will to force myself to turn around. From the sound, I expected wolves. What I found was much worse.

Cerberus. A canine, to be sure. But Cerberus was no forest-dwelling wolf. Five times the size of even the largest wolves roving the forests of my father's lands, but that wasn't the worst of it. It was stocky, rippled with thick muscles, its neck wide and squat. And atop that neck... five heads. Saliva dripped from heavy jowls, its bared teeth each the size of my palm.

The color drained from my face as its eyes, red as Aphrodite's smoke, focused on me. I backed up several steps, moving slowly in the hopes it would not give chase, but a scream ripped from my throat with my next step back as something cold brushed my spine. The touch was frigid, icier than the breath of Borealis, but the pressure was firm. Fingers, I realized, which traced lightly along my neck before coming to rest on my shoulder.

"You come before your time," a deep yet feminine voice said, close to my ear. "Warm breath still raises a mist from your lips, and your heart thunders loud enough to rouse jealousy in the sleeping dead, my dear."

Persephone. I reeled around to face her. She stood an arm's length away, her profile to me. I gave her my most gracious smile, trying to keep the salivating many-headed dog in my peripheral vision. "Persephone. They did not lie when they spoke of your beauty."

These words were true. She was, indeed, breathtaking, just as Aphrodite had claimed, but in a wildly different way from the Goddess of Beauty. Crimson hair, the color of spilled blood, hung long and loose, swept over her slender shoulder. Calm radiated from Persephone, a stillness that bordered on sullenness. She did not turn to face me, only flicked her dark eyes up to meet my gaze and frowned.

Her frown was immediate and tight. "Surely you did not come to the realm of the dead to flatter me?"

I shook my head, unable to form words.

Unimpressed by my response, she went on. "Give me one good reason why I should not feed you to Cerberus." Her one visible eye broke off my gaze, moving towards where I knew the hell hound loomed.

I gave her a wistful shake of the head and found my words. "No. I am here on an errand."

Persephone's head cocked to one side. "A mortal with hot blood and living breath on an errand in Hade's realm? For whom?"

Honesty, they say, is always the best policy. And while this might not be true in every situation, even I was wise enough to know not to lie to the bride of Hades.

"Aphrodite." The name of our shared nemesis fell off my lips.

Persephone's face remained unmoved, but she stiffened almost imperceptibly. "Only a fool speaks that name in my domain." Her tone was flat, making me wonder just what it would take to move her and just how terrifying she would be if she let the mask of her indifference slip into rage.

Her gaze shifted slightly, darting behind me. Remembering the hellhound lingering behind me, I quickly continued. "Persephone, there is no love lost between Aphrodite and me. But I must do her bidding if I wish to ever see my husband again."

With this, she arched a brow. "You are the one, then? The mortal girl who wed Eros. They said your beauty rivals Aphrodite's beauty. It is untrue."

I took the insult in stride and gave her a wry smile. "I know. It was my father who said this, not I. I never tried to compete with any Goddess in beauty or anything else. But yes, I am that girl. My name is Psyche." I humbled myself to her, and it seemed to have the desired effect. Her face softened ever so slightly.

"Tell me why you heed Aphrodite's bidding. Only a fool would venture into the Underworld while still alive."

A sigh escaped my lips. I was loath to relive the miseries I'd endured, but I recanted them to the Mistress of the underworld all the same. I told her about my cruel father and how he treated me like a chip to bargain with rather than a young girl. I told her of Apollo and his dire tidings, my time with Eros, spent in darkness, believing him a monster, but giving him my heart, anyway.

"But in the end," I went on, "I betrayed him. I looked upon his face despite all the warnings." I lowered my eyes, my cheeks burning with shame. "And coming here"—I gestured to the desolation surrounding us—"is the only chance I stand to win him back and prove I'm worthy of him."

Persephone studied me with an unreadable sideways gaze, then turned to face me at last. The left side of her face came into view, a death's head, gleaming bone white with only a black chasm where her eye ought to be. A grave worm wriggled out, winding from the empty socket into the fleshless hole of her nostril.

I recoiled, and she responded with a steady, humorless expression. "You find my duality repulsive, but I assure you, the same is within you. It may not mar your pretty face, but it is there, just beneath the flesh. There can be no light without darkness. No life without its eventual demise."

I averted my eyes, my cheeks coloring with shame. "It was unexpected. That is all. I see the beauty of both sides."

That was, perhaps, a bit of a lie.

She sighed and shook her head as if I had missed the point. "What precisely do you need from me? To appease the bitter and jealous Aphrodite and win back your true love?"

"A sliver of your beauty," I replied in a quiet voice.

Persephone nodded, setting her chin as if she'd made up her mind. The grave worm emerged then darted back into her hollow eye with the motion of her head. "Your plea has not fallen on deaf ears."

With a wave of her hand, a small box appeared. It was varnished in black and engraved with skulls entwined with flowers. Persephone held it out to me. "Here, give this to Aphrodite. A sliver of the beauty of the underworld."

There was something sharp in her voice that made me nervous. The box made my skin crawl. I did not want to touch it. All of my synapses screamed for me to run from the Mistress of the Dead and whatever lay enclosed in the container she held.

But Eros, a longing voice in my mind whispered.

I reached out and took the box. Just as my fingers closed around it, there was a sudden flash of light, and a burst of warmth as the Goddess of Beauty appeared. Persephone's cold gaze turned on Aphrodite at once.

"You are not welcome in my domain," Persephone said. She was calm as ever, but her lips had turned down in a deep frown, and the grave worm moved around more animatedly as if compelled by her hidden anger.

Aphrodite glanced at her and rolled her eyes. "I'll only be a minute," she snapped. Then she turned to me.

"Do you have it?" the words rushed out of her mouth. She seemed somehow different than before, agitated, impatient. Her power bleeding off her in erratic bursts.

I nodded and outstretched my hands to Aphrodite, but she threw both hands up as if in defense. "No, you open it," she said with a jerk of her chin.

Persephone's eyes flicked to me, and she shook her head slowly as if in a warning. I studied the box. It pulsed with a darkness that filled me with dread. Then to Aphrodite, who fidgeted, shifting her weight from one foot to the other.

"Come now," she wheedled. "You've come so far, accomplished so much. Will you really give it all up now? Or will you open the box and gaze upon what lays within? It is your only chance to see Eros again."

I had to open it. For Eros. For the new life I held inside me, the Demigod that was part of both of us. My hands shook as I lifted the small clasp with a soft click. I slid my finger under the lip and began prying it back. I had only opened it a crevice when a voice I would know anywhere boomed through the stagnant air of the Underworld.

"Psyche, don't!"

I was so startled that my hand jerked, flinging the box wide. I tried to look away, to seek the face of my husband, who had just cried out to me. But I could not. The contents of the box emerged in a blinding plume of grave dust. It poured down my throat through my agape mouth to choke me.

I stared into the void. And when it beckoned to me, and I was helpless to deny its call.

❧ 18 ❧

INTERLUDE

THE GODDESS OF BEAUTY WATCHED AS THE CLOUD OF grave dust spewed forth from the box, coating her son's lover. A sliver of Persephone's beauty, it was to be sure, but it was the dark side. The blackness, the decay, the rot, and release from the toils of the world. Persephone had given Psyche a handful of death locked within that little box, most assuredly intended for Aphrodite herself. But Aphrodite would never have been fool enough to open the dread thing. Though, as an immortal, it would not have killed her, as it would a mortal. It would have marred her beauty, which was even worse.

Barely containing a victorious smile, she watched as her son's mortal lover collapsed to the dusty gray soil. Psyche's body writhed, twisting and contorting as she gasped desperately for air that would not come. Her fair hair and ivory skin went pale, then turned gray, colorless, as all things in the Underworld were.

Eros fell to the ground at his mortal wife's side and pulled her body into his arms. He smoothed her graying hair back from her brow and ran his fingers along the smooth curve of her cheek. Cold, so cold, was that warm flesh he had touched a thousand times before in lust and in love. His shattered wail sliced the unnatural silence of the Underworld, carrying to the far corners of the realm where it was heard by Mighty Zeus, who had ventured below to see what trouble his wayward daughter had caused now.

Lightning cut through the sky, the smell of ozone filling the air and assaulting the senses of the deities surrounding the weeping God who clung to Psyche's corpse, which no longer convulsed but only twitched periodically.

"What is the meaning of this?" Zeus demanded, slamming his Thunderbolt to the ground. The earth quaked, and all three deities clustered around Psyche collapsed to their knees.

Curses burned unspoken on Aphrodite's tongue. There was only one who could undo the fate her son's mortal wife had embraced; her father, king amongst the Gods, who stood before them now. Eros did not so much as look up at Zeus when he spoke. His head was pressed to Psyche's cheek, breathing in the sweet scent of her that was slipping away with her life force.

And so it was Persephone, Mistress of the Underworld, who spoke.

"It was not yet her time. This was yet another of Aphrodite's cruel plots." Her eyes cast daggers at the Goddess of Beauty, who jutted her chin out defiantly.

"The girl agreed to the terms I set before her. Her downfall was her own doing. She betrayed my son."

Persephone shrugged, "She told me what you did." She turned to face Zeus with the beautiful side of her face, leaving her death's head to leer at Aphrodite. The grave worm slinking out of its lair within her eye socket and stretching out as if it would strangle the Goddess of Beauty if it could. "This girl was an innocent. A victim all her life. Aphrodite stole from her the only love she had ever known. And this"—she gestured at Psyche's prone, colorless form—"is the result of her scheming."

A scowl crossed Zeus' face as his gaze fell on his daughter. "Where does this jealous spitefulness in you come from? The nymph's blood of your mother? Surely not from me," he snapped before directing his attention to the weeping form of Eros.

"Eros," he began, "what would right this wrong?"

Eros blinked up at him, tears flowing freely. "Bring her back."

Zeus huffed, crossing his massive arms across his barrel chest. "You know there is only one way to do that," he chided.

Eros ran his fingers along Psyche's parted lips, through which breath no longer fell. He passed his hand over her sightless, once blue eyes, now gone gray. "She has earned it!"

"No!" Aphrodite gasped, a sharp intake of breath. "You cannot give her immortality! That was her goal all along!"

Eros looked up at his mother, his eyes shifting to a deep, impenetrable blue in his fury. "That is a lie! All she wanted was me, and I could never fully give myself to her because of you and your plots and insecurities. *You did this! You killed her.* Mother, I swear, if this is not made right, if I cannot bring her back, I will bring a wrath you have never seen down on your head."

With his words, Eros rose, unslinging his bow from his shoulder, causing Aphrodite's eyes to go wide with alarm. Persephone stood by, an ever-so-faint smile on her lips as she watched the Goddess of Beauty squirm.

"STOP!" Zeus boomed, and all eyes returned to him. He lowered his voice to barely more than a whisper, directing it at Eros. "Do you love her? Would you have her for eternity?"

"I love her more than words can say, and eternity is not

enough time. From the moment I saw her, I knew she was destined for me. The fates intended us to be one. We are two halves of the same whole." His voice was soft, his eyes pleading.

"Then use your Godhead to restore her."

Aphrodite let loose a desperate, furious shriek, but Zeus moved quickly, taking her by the arm. "No more from you, daughter. Let this be a lesson to you about your ceaseless meddling and your eternal envy. Come with me and leave your son to his happiness, for once."

He did not wait for a response. There was a sharp crack of thunder as lightning slashed, both Zeus and Aphrodite disappearing into the bright hole it rent in the sky.

Persephone gave Eros an acquiescing nod of her head. "It was not yet her time," she said, then turned and wandered away with slow steps back into the eternal gray that was her winter world.

Eros bent down, pressing his lips gently against his wife's.

❧ 19 ❧

IMMORTALITY

WARMTH. IT FILLED MY BODY, A TINGLING HEAT THAT began at my lips and coursed down through my throat, into my limbs and my core. There was a jolt in my heart, which must have been the moment it began beating anew, and a fluttering in my belly—my child.

My eyes flew open, and the first thing I saw was his face. The aquiline nose, the unblemished bronze skin that seemed to radiate light itself, the stray curl falling across his brow, hiding one cerulean eye. I reached up and tucked the lock of hair back behind his ear.

"Psyche," he whispered, his voice husky, and my heart sang.

"Eros!" I threw my arms around him, pulling him close, burying my face in his neck, and breathing in the wind and rain scent of him. He returned the embrace so tightly I thought he might shatter me.

When he released me, I sat up and noticed something had changed. I could not put my finger on what, at first. I only knew I felt stronger, lighter as if new blood was coursing through my veins.

"What happened?" I asked, blinking at the gray world around me, which I saw through new eyes.

"Now we can be together forever, as we were fated to be," he whispered, his breath tickling the sensitive place at the back of my ear.

"Forever?"

"For all eternity. Just you and me."

I realized then what he meant. He had given me the gift of immortality. I, the girl who for so many years played a charade of divinity, was now a Goddess. The fates worked in strange ways, but it seemed they were not always as cruel as I had believed they were.

I shook my head. "No. You will have to share me," I whispered, a mischievous glimmer in my eyes.

He blinked at me and cocked his head, confused. And I took his hand and brought it to my abdomen, pressing it lightly against the slightly distended flesh there.

"We will call her Hedone," I said, watching as realization dawned, his eyes widening as a smile tugged at her lips. "And her life will be everything that mine was not."

www.ingramcontent.com/pod-product-compliance
Lightning Source LLC
Chambersburg PA
CBHW052004170626
46808CB00007B/2771